Out of the FIRE

AJ RANNEY

Rudy House Publishing

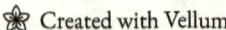

To every Violet out there who is strong, confident, and sometimes a little bit different.

Listen on Spotify!

Settlin' - Sugarland
Feels Like This - Abra Taylor
Wildfire - Ava Pearfecto
When the Party's Over - Billie Eilish
Fire Fire - Shimza, AR/CO, Kasango
How Bad Do U Want Me - Lady Gaga
Dark Romance - TfamilyRocky
Tell Me I'm Pretty - Ava Pearfecto
Pretty Distraction - SkyDxddy
She Rises and She Glows - Linhy
Power - The Score
Wild Eyes - Alivan Blu
Gettin' Warmed Up - Jason Aldean
Something Good - Tim Halperin
Still Falling For You - Ellie Goulding

Chapter One

SETH

WHY WAS this dude so damn happy all the time? I narrowed my eyes at Zack's back, hoping he could feel my gaze burning into him. Did he have to sing all the fucking time?

I'd been with the Half Moon Lake Fire Department since April, and the guys as a whole were a pretty decent crew. They'd slowly grown on me, but now it was August and some days I still wanted to throttle Zack and the rays of sunshine that shot out of his ass. I couldn't understand how someone could possibly be that... I didn't even have a word for it. He reminded me of that troll with pink hair from that movie my niece used to watch on repeat.

Shit. I needed to remember to call my brother and wish my niece Dani a happy birthday. She'd be heartbroken if I didn't.

Moving out of Charlotte was the right decision, and while the drive back home was less than two hours, I was still struggling not seeing them as often as I used to.

I turned back to the current game of rummy we were all playing. Jay Mitchell, the youngest guy on the crew, laid down a set of threes. Attempting to tune out Zack's incessant singing, I assessed the cards in my hand before pulling a six and adding it to my run already on the table.

"You really hate the singing, don't you?" Jay cocked a brow and a slight smirk pulled at his lips.

"I don't understand how it doesn't bother any of you."

Jay shrugged. "I think at this point we're just used to it."

I still didn't get it. But Jay had a two-year-old kid and recently found out he had another one on the way, so maybe he was overly conditioned to unnecessary noise.

Adam chuckled next to me as he laid down a run of four. "We've learned and accepted that Zack is going to be who he is."

Still contemplating how that translated to tuning Zach out, I ran my fingers over the short beard that lined my jaw. It needed a trim. I'd been surprised to find that this station was more lenient with the no-beard policy than most firehouses were. Even the one I'd been at in Charlotte enforced it. It was one of the things I hated. A beard suited me, but I understood the policy. Here though, as long as I could pass a fit test with my mask, I could keep the beard. It required maintenance and trimming, but it was a solid trade-off. The same rule applied to long hair. As long as I could tie it back or secure it under my helmet, I was good to go.

The chair across from me scraped along the floor as our driver, Logan Murray, pulled it out and sat down. "What are we talking about?"

"Zack," Jay offered. "And his singing."

Logan scoffed. "Don't forget the dancing."

Everyone snickered in unison. Except me. I didn't find it funny. Only annoying.

Don't get me wrong, the dude was a solid firefighter. I had no issue with him. When he wasn't singing or dancing or hopping around like the fucking Energizer bunny.

Adam stiffened in his spot next to me, and I followed his gaze to Lyla—our newest EMT—who'd just exited from the bunk room and was headed down the stairs. She'd been at the station over a month, and even though Adam repeatedly denied liking her, it hadn't stopped the guys from giving him shit about it. I didn't really know the dude that well and even I could tell he was into her.

"You gonna ask her out yet?" Logan cocked a brow.

Adam narrowed his eyes. "No. Like I've told you before, we're just friends."

"I heard she's dating someone." Jay leaned back in his chair and laced his hands behind his head.

"Yep." Adam looked back down, staring intently at his cards.

That one word had so much more behind it, but I had to give the guy credit. He was doing a decent job masking his reaction to Jay's comment.

The lights on the PA system lit up and we all threw down our cards and pushed our chairs back knowing a call was coming in. The shrill sound of the alarm blasted through the station as we made our way down to the bay.

I mentally reviewed who was where as we went through our routine of stepping into our boots and pulling on our turnout gear. Adam was paired with Lyla today as EMTs, so it was just Logan, Jay, Zack, and me in the rig. Being part of such a small crew was also something I had to get used to. In Charlotte, our shifts consisted of at least eight, sometimes ten people per team. That was a double-edged sword. The larger house and consistent calls kept my mind and body busy, but at the end of a twelve—sometimes twenty-four—hour shift, I was socially exhausted.

Owen, our lieutenant—who was also being groomed to take over as chief once ours retired—headed out first in one of the utility trucks.

"That's the old Miller farm," Logan announced as he climbed up into the driver's seat and started the engine on the quint.

"Crap. Hasn't that been abandoned for the last few years?" Jay asked.

"Yup." Logan pulled the rig out of the bay and switched on the sirens.

I'd actually never seen a quint truck in action before moving here. In Charlotte we had a pumper and a separate aerial ladder truck. But the combination one they had here made sense for a smaller, more rural station.

Adam and Lyla followed behind in the bus. We were all silent, listening to dispatch and Owen communicate, hoping it wasn't our arsonist starting up again. Even I was getting tired of his shit, and I'd only been dealing with it since I'd moved to Half Moon Lake in April. These guys had been dealing with it since January.

We'd all breathed a sigh of relief when it stopped after Logan's garage was set on fire. But now tension hung in the air as we made our way to another fire that might have been set intentionally.

Once on scene, Owen dished out commands, sending Jay and me in for the primary search and leaving Logan and Zack to start getting water on the fire.

The farmhouse was a small two-story home and the fire had moved quickly, making visibility difficult. After quickly searching the ground level, Jay radioed back.

"First floor clear, heading up to second."

We finished our search, finding no one, and made our way back downstairs. By then, two more trucks from neighboring towns had pulled up to assist.

I didn't want to voice what was going through my head, but I knew I had to. Owen needed to know what we were dealing with. We still needed to complete the overhaul process, making sure there was no burning inside the walls of the farmhouse that could rekindle and create additional issues. But I'd been doing this for almost eight years now—since becoming a firefighter at twenty-one—working in a busy station, and I'd dealt with my fair share of intentionally set fires.

During the primary search of the farmhouse, the first thing I noticed was some of the burning was happening along the floor rather than the ceiling. In my experience, that pattern was typically seen when an accelerant was used. And an accelerant in an abandoned home was rarely, if ever, accidental or natural.

Although I was sure I wasn't, I prayed I was wrong.

Chapter Two

VIOLET

It had been two months. Two months of quiet. But now the arsonist was back at it? Why?

I shook my head and looked around at the guys starting their overhaul process. The Half Moon Lake Police Department had been working jointly with the state fire investigators to help catch the arsonist. So far, with no luck. Being the PD's only crime scene tech, I was pulled in to assist after Logan found a matchbook at one of the scenes. And since the state wasn't sending anyone to help until we had more evidence to provide them, I was the only one responsible for collecting and examining evidence found at the scenes, as well as viewing any video footage collected. Yay for job security, but it was a lot for one person to manage. That was small-town life.

"That's bullshit." Logan glared at Dylan, who was not only a detective with Half Moon Lake PD but also Logan's neighbor and friend.

I understood why Logan was pissed. I wasn't happy either when the guy we were looking at alibied out of one of the fires. And he hadn't tried setting *my* house on fire. Okay, technically it was Logan's garage, but still. It was close enough to his house that he deserved to be pissed.

"I agree." Dylan crossed his arms over his chest. "But there's not much we can do about it right now. We're working on trying to piece everything together. Maybe it's him, maybe it's someone else. Maybe he's working with someone."

We were all sure it was the kid they pulled from a fire seven years ago. Motive was easy to pinpoint—he blamed the Half Moon Lake FD for the death of his father. But without hard evidence, and considering he technically had an alibi for one of the fires, possibly a second we were still looking into, there was literally nothing we could do to him. Granted, the time on ring cameras could be easily altered if you knew what you were doing, so I wasn't sure how airtight that alibi would be. But until we could prove otherwise, that alibi stuck.

I'd already looked around the two rooms that faced the front of the house. I noted burn patterns similar to those in the other fires that would indicate an accelerant was poured. I'd also collected remnants from one spot that was likely from a book of matches, just like in the other fires.

I made my way to the entryway that led to the kitchen, letting the guys continue to talk about our suspect, or technically, our lack of one.

"Oh." I stumbled back as a large body stepped into the doorway, blocking my path.

I smiled. *Mountain Man.* I'd bestowed that nickname on Seth Davis the first time I'd met him. Rugged, burly, bearded, with long reddish-brown hair to match. He even lived up on the mountain, rarely seen by anyone. Almost mythical, like Bigfoot or Paul Bunyan. Truthfully, I wasn't even sure if he talked.

"Sorry," I said when he made no attempt to move. "Need to look around the kitchen."

He dipped his head and grunted, stepping to the side and letting me pass through the archway. Without another word, he exited the same way I came in.

He was strange, but people thought I was strange too, and I was perfectly normal. I had an affinity for the color black and preferred to decorate with skulls. What was wrong with that? I was also a firm believer that a really good pair of fishnets went with any outfit.

That, paired with my white and black hair and piercings, had definitely given me a label around town. Back in Asheville, where I lived post-graduation before taking the job here, no one batted an eye. People complimented me on my unique style. Here in Half Moon Lake? Not so much.

I popped in my other earbud and tapped it, cueing up my dark pop playlist.

Finished in the kitchen, I carefully made my way upstairs. I doubted I would find anything on the second floor, but I wouldn't be doing my job if I didn't inspect as much as I could.

I finished in the second bedroom and spun, ready to move on, but froze suddenly as the smell of smoke hit my nose. Not ash or the smell of char. Smoke. Like from an active fire.

As I stepped back into the hallway, I immediately began coughing. Thick smoke wafted up the staircase and filled the space around me. Crap. That wasn't good.

I coughed again before turning and going back into the bedroom, closing the door behind me. There was nothing in this room for me to put under the door to prevent the smoke from seeping in, and of course the windows had to be boarded up. No escape there.

It was fine. The guys would put out the fire that must have relit and come searching for me.

They had to know I was up here, right?

SETH

"Where's Violet?" Dylan looked around at the group of us assembled at the standard checkpoint in front of the farmhouse. The fire had reignited in the front room while we were overhauling the kitchen. Definitely not what we were hoping for.

"What do you mean?" Did she not come out with the rest of us? A quick glance around confirmed she wasn't out here. No one could miss the fishnets and shiny black shorts she wore.

"She was in there." Dylan tipped his head toward the house.

No shit. We all saw her. But the problem was she wasn't out here with the rest of us.

"You're sure?" Owen asked. "Mitchell, you said no one else was inside."

"There wasn't." Jay nodded to the second floor. "Unless she went upstairs."

Christ. Standing here arguing about where she might have gone wasn't solving anything. The fire blocked the front room already, and the windows were boarded up, so if she was on the second floor, she wasn't getting out that way.

I turned back to the truck and grabbed the Halligan, avoiding the guys grabbing the hoses to have a second go at the stubborn flames.

"Davis," Owen's voice boomed as I ran toward the front door.

I would likely get my ass handed to me for this, but I couldn't

18

just stand around. With everything being so hot and unstable from the original burning, it wouldn't take long for the fire to make it to the second level.

I held my breath as I entered the house. The flames were just beginning to lap at the stairs as I ascended them. Visibility on the second floor wasn't great, but getting down low made it a little better. I went left to check the master bedroom first. After calling out and performing a quick but thorough search, including the attached bathroom, I headed back into the hallway. The smoke was thicker and it was getting harder to see. But the first thing I noticed as I made my way down the hallway toward the other rooms was that all the doors were ajar except for one.

Good girl.

I pushed it open and stepped inside, closing it behind me. She was huddled in the furthest corner from the door.

"Mountain Man," she whispered and stood with a smile.

What the fuck did she just say? I narrowed my eyes at her and then assessed the room.

"Let's go," I called and made my way to one of the windows that faced the front. I was sure the flames would be at the stairs by now. Best option was to get the boards off and go out that way.

The faint sound of wood splintering followed by a loud crash reverberated through the room. *Fuck.* That wasn't good. We needed to get out. Now.

I used the Halligan to pry the wood away from the window casing and leaned out to get my bearings.

"There," Jay yelled. "Get the ladder."

I turned back toward Violet just as all the blood drained from her face.

"What's wrong?"

"Nothing." She squared her shoulders and flinched when the ladder clamored loudly against the siding.

I waved toward the window. "You go first."

She started to shake her head then stopped, but she still didn't make any attempt to move.

"We gotta go. You'll be fine. I'll be right behind you."

"I'm, umm... afraid of heights."

Fucking great. Did that mean she wasn't planning to go out the window? Because being burned by fire seemed like a much less appealing alternative.

"Like I get all dizzy and lightheaded and might have a panic attack afraid of heights."

I stomped to the window. Couldn't just leave her there. And even if they got the fire out, I didn't think the stairs would be any good at this point.

I climbed out on the ladder and reached my hand back inside toward her. "Come."

She raised an eyebrow, but tentatively moved toward the window.

"Close your eyes," I added.

"How am I supposed to climb down with my eyes closed?"

"I'll direct you. Just don't open your eyes."

"You guys coming down or what?" Jay hollered from the ground where he held the ladder. Logan and Zack were already applying water to the far side of the house, and I knew we were running out of time before they needed to hit close to where we were at.

But I ignored him as Violet's tiny hand landed in my large palm. I helped guide her through the window until she was seated on the windowsill, level with the ladder.

"Spread your legs." The words came out husky and I cursed internally. I'd carried women down ladders a shit ton of times. But not exactly like this. This was definitely not a standard carry. Those were intended for use with victims who were unconscious or hurt, and Violet was neither.

She smirked, but kept her eyes closed and did as I asked. Maybe I'd be better off just throwing her over my shoulder, but having her in front of me would give me more balance going down. And this was the only way I could think that would stop her from opening her eyes and freaking out on the ladder, which could bring us both down—and not in a good way.

"I'm going to pull you toward me. When I do, wrap your legs and arms around me. Got it?"

"Like a monkey?"

I huffed. "Yeah. Like a monkey."

She chuckled hesitantly. "Okay."

I gripped her waist, trying to ignore the brush of her fingers against my skin and how the hair on the back of my neck prickled with electricity as she wrapped her arms around me. The moment I pulled her against me, securing her tightly around my front, I regretted my choice.

The guys were convinced getting laid would help my grumpy disposition. I had no problem with who I was, but they might be on to something, regardless of why. It had been far too long since I'd had a woman in my bed. And given my reaction to the one wrapped around my body, it was safe to say I needed to make that a priority in the near future.

I held her tightly against me with one hand and climbed slowly down the ladder, holding it with my other hand.

Once my feet hit the ground, I spun. "You can let go now."

"Oh," she squeaked. "Right."

Her legs released their death grip on me and she slid them down to the ground.

The sound of people clapping had us both turning toward a small crowd gathered at the safety perimeter. What the fuck? Where did all these people come from? And why? I flinched when someone held up their phone. Jesus. She better not be taking pictures. That was the last thing I needed. I left Charlotte and moved here to avoid that shit.

I caught Owen's glare aimed at me. What did he want me to do? Sit around and wait?

That wasn't me. I'd rather ask for forgiveness than permission. Especially when someone's life was potentially at risk.

Violet swayed on her feet and instinct had me reaching out, wrapping an arm around her back. "Come on." I turned her toward the ambulance. "You need to be checked out."

"I'm fine."

I shook my head. Fine my ass. But she could argue with Adam and Lyla. She was their problem now.

Chapter Three

SETH

IT WAS FUCKING RIDICULOUS. In the days following me carrying Violet out of the farmhouse, half a dozen women had shown up at the station. All bringing me stuff and asking if I'm single. Some lunatic even gave me her panties.

Apparently, some lady posted a video of me getting Violet out of the window and climbing down the ladder with her wrapped around my front. And of course it went viral. The caption read *Save a ladder, climb a firefighter* for fuck's sake.

Comments were ridiculous. Some even crude. Not that it offended me. But I just wanted to be left the fuck alone.

I'd moved here from Charlotte because I hated the limelight. Now I had to deal with it here too? In a big city, and with our house having the first female battalion chief, we were under a microscope.

Anything we did, people either wanted to criticize or idolize. The final straw for me was when we saved the life of a famous actor after he'd acted like an idiot and drove his car into a tree. At first, the attention was all positive. Then he started bad-mouthing us. He was pissed we'd told the cops his breath reeked of alcohol. Eventually the full story came out and people stopped attacking us. But those months of dealing with the drama had been frustrating to say the least.

I crossed my arms over my chest and spun to head back upstairs. I swear, if one more woman showed up, I was going to lose my damn mind.

"Another one?" Jay snickered, stopping me before I could climb to the safety of the second level. He was standing with Owen and Logan while they were doing an equipment check.

"Yeah." At least I was able to turn away her tray of brownies with a made-up nut allergy. I tilted my head. I'd been here four months and never saw any of these guys dealing with this kind of shit. "How come they don't bother you guys?"

"What?" Logan's brows pulled together. "You mean the women?"

"Yeah. Do you guys not do heroic shit? Are you *that* useless or something?"

Jay scoffed. "No, we're just *that* taken."

"Taken?"

"Yeah." Jay held up his left hand and Owen followed suit, both showing their wedding bands. "We're married. And everyone in town knows it."

"And I don't have a wedding band yet, but everyone knows I'm dating his sister." Logan hitched his thumb toward Jay.

Jay rolled his eyes. "Don't remind me."

"So if I was taken, they would leave me alone?"

It couldn't possibly be that easy. Maybe I could show everyone a picture of Lucy and me and tell them she was my girlfriend from back home. It was close enough to the truth. They didn't have to know she was my *ex*-girlfriend.

But all of that would require me to talk to these women. I didn't want to talk to anyone.

Maybe I could hire someone.

"I don't want her to look like a prostitute," I pondered, bringing my hand up and running it down my jaw.

"What?" Owen asked with one brow raised. "Why are we talking about hookers now?"

"We aren't. That's the point. No hookers. That wouldn't work."

Jay shook his head with a scoff. "I think we're missing part of this conversation you're having with yourself."

I shook my head. "Don't worry about it."

"Oh, look. Here comes the damsel herself." Logan chuckled as he tipped his chin over my shoulder.

I spun to find Violet approaching. What the fuck was she wearing now? Fishnets, a pink and black plaid skirt, and some type of tank top that laced up in the front and made her tits look like they were going to spill out at any minute.

My feet were moving toward her before I even realized what I was doing.

As I stopped in front of her, she held up a Tupperware container. "I made you cookies."

"Jesus, not you too." I groaned. "I don't need cookies." Or anything else for that matter. I was just doing my fucking job.

She shrugged, a smile still plastered on her face. "I wanted to do something to thank you."

"Thank me?"

"Yeah, you know, for saving my life and everything."

I opened my mouth to respond, but glared over her shoulder as another woman began walking up from the street toward us. Grabbing Violet's hand, I pulled her further into the station and then glanced back. The strange woman had stopped, and she looked pissed.

Good. So was I.

I looked over at the guys who were once again focused on checking the equipment. Maybe they were on to something.

Only one way to find out. I stepped forward and wrapped my arms around Violet, bringing her in for a hug.

For someone who looked like Wednesday from the *Addams Family,* I was surprised that she smelled like a field of sunflowers on a summer day. A mix of honey, grass, and a light floral scent.

That same feeling I had when she wrapped around me on the ladder was back. Soft, surprisingly pleasant.

She wrapped her arms around my back. "Would have never guessed you were a hugger. But you're in luck, 'cause I give the best hugs. Or so I've been told."

The strange woman turned and walked away. Interesting.

I untangled myself and stepped back. "You said you wanted to thank me?"

"Yeah." She squeaked before clearing her throat and lifting the container again. "Cookies."

"I need a girlfriend."

She tilted her head. "A girlfriend?"

"Yeah. I need it to stop."

"Need what to stop?" Her brows pulled together. Had she not seen the video that blew up?

"The women. They won't leave me alone after that video was posted."

"Oh. That. Yeah, those comments are hilarious."

"You want to thank me? Pretend you're my girlfriend so everyone will leave me alone."

"But, I baked you cookies." She thrust the container out toward me. "Remember?"

I shook my head. "I don't eat sugar."

Her lips formed a pout and I could see her mind working. Good, that meant she was at least considering it.

"How would that even work?" I sensed more curiosity than hesitance in her voice. Another good sign. "You can't just tell people that. They'd expect to see us around town together and stuff."

"I'll take you out." What the hell did I just say? And why? I didn't want to have to talk to anyone. But I guess if I had to choose, Violet didn't seem like she'd be horrible company.

She smiled brightly. "Like on a date?"

Christ. I narrowed my eyes. Last thing I needed was her getting the wrong idea. "Fake date," I clarified.

"Right." She glanced up, thinking it over before finally shrugging. "Okay. Fine. When?"

Perfect. One date. That should be enough to solve my problem. "Tomorrow night."

"Will you bring me flowers?"

I glowered at her. "No."

She huffed. "Will you at least try my cookies?"

Shit, if she was going to help me keep these women away, I'd eat the entire container.

"Fine. I'll try the damn cookies."

She popped open the container and I took one out, shoving the entire thing in my mouth. "Not bad," I mumbled around the chewy combination of sugar coma ingredients. They were actually pretty good.

"You have a phone, Mountain Man?"

She had called me that in the house when I stepped into the room. "Don't call me that." I pulled out my phone and handed it to her.

"Well, if we're fake dating, we have to have pet names for each other. It's either Mountain Man or Pookie. Your choice," she said with a pep I didn't share and then began entering her phone number into my phone.

Maybe this was a bad idea. Because I was sure this chick was going to drive me insane.

Chapter Four

VIOLET

WHAT THE HELL had I agreed to? I shut the door to my car and sat in the driver's seat, staring back at the gruff man who'd just asked me to pretend to be his girlfriend. I thought that kind of stuff only happened in books.

My phone chimed with a notification and I picked it up, groaning at the text from my ex.

This whole thing with Seth might actually work out well. Ever since my "near death" experience, as my ex called it, he'd been trying desperately to get back together. I had absolutely no interest. Finding him with another woman destroyed any chance of that. I didn't care that he realized he'd made a mistake. And if I made it clear I'd moved on with someone else, maybe he would leave me alone.

Before I could type out a reply, Dylan's name flashed across my screen and I slid the answer button over. "What's up, bossman?"

He scoffed. "Are you ever gonna call me Dylan?"

"Nope." I smiled. There was just something about nicknames that brought a smile to my face, and I only used them for people I liked.

"The fire investigators have asked us to do a deep dive into the Taylors. See if there's anyone else connected to the family who could be a suspect."

I sat up straighter. Was he serious? "Does that mean we're done looking at the kid?"

"For now." He was quiet. It didn't feel right, and I knew he felt it too. "My hands are tied at this point. He has at least one solid alibi. The only thing we can do is figure out if someone's helping him, or if there's someone else holding a grudge."

Logically, I understood what he was saying. But my gut didn't like it. "Fine. I'm on my way in. Be there in five."

Arson was one of the most difficult crimes to solve. Evidence from the scenes was almost nonexistent. At least evidence that could point to a suspect. What we needed was a witness. But so far he was good about going unnoticed.

"I thought you were grabbing breakfast with Hattie?"

"It's ok. I can reschedule." I'd become good friends with Dylan's fiancée over the last six months. I didn't have many local friends since taking the job and moving to Half Moon Lake two years ago. But after Hattie picked up a stalker earlier this year, and Dylan stepped in to protect her while we solved the case, we became friends.

"No. Go to breakfast. I know Hattie was looking forward to it."

"You sure?"

"Yeah. I'll start digging. I'll catch you up when you get here."

"Okay."

I was dying to tell Hattie what just happened with Seth. But first I had to bring someone else up to speed on this latest development.

Hanging up with Dylan, I opened the text from my ex and began typing a response.

> Me: I'm dating someone now. Please stop texting me.

There. That should do it. And if he didn't believe me, someone was bound to see me at dinner with Seth and news would spread. Small-town gossip to save the day.

I RUBBED MY TEMPLES. Dylan and I had been digging through anyone who had any connection to our suspect's family all day. My eyes were starting to cross.

They were a straightforward family. Dad was a self-employed plumber. Mom helped with the bookkeeping of the business. Two sons, eight years apart. Youngest son was pulled from his family's house fire seven years ago while the older brother was away at college. Parents were rescued as well, but the dad was rushed to the hospital for smoke inhalation. He'd died last year from pneumonia, and looking at his health history, it looked like he'd had respiratory issues consistently over the past seven years since the fire. But he was also a smoker before the fire ever happened. And who knows if he actually quit or kept smoking after the fire.

The oldest son didn't live locally. He was a dentist in Ohio. Neither the mom nor dad had much family here. Mom was from Florida; the rest of her family was still living there. Dad was local, but an only child, both of his parents having passed away years earlier.

"I think I got it." Dylan's voice broke through my thoughts. I spun my chair and raised a brow at the manila folder in his hand. "Who is most likely to be an arsonist?"

Great. Profiling. My favorite topic of choice. "You know how I feel about this."

"Yes, Violet. I know. But humor me. Because we can't ignore statistics."

I sighed. "Fine. Young white males."

"So our twenty-year-old with a possible grudge against the Half Moon Lake FD is the perfect suspect, right?"

I nodded.

"But what are new studies indicating most serial arsonists do for a living?"

"Firefighters." It was why they were harder to catch. They knew how to not get caught. I shrugged. "But since it hasn't been tracked, there's no way to know the exact percentage."

Dylan stepped forward and handed me the folder in his hand.

I opened it and skimmed the information. "He's older."

"Probably why the investigators haven't considered him."

"Retired firefighter." I continued to peruse his details before looking up at Dylan. "Connected to the Taylors?"

He nodded. "He's the boys' godfather."

"So are we thinking they're working together?"

Dylan pursed his lips and shook his head. "I think we play this as a new suspect. Let's see if we can connect him to any of the fires, starting with the locations. I might have a chat with him tomorrow about the kid to see if I can get a read on him."

He was right, we couldn't keep fixating on the son. Not with him having at least one airtight alibi. Camera footage from the convenience store verified he was nowhere near the BBQ joint when it burned down in May. The same location where Logan had found the book of matches that led us to the Taylors to begin with.

"I want to go back to the beginning," Dylan continued. "Going to ask the captain if I can pull some guys. Canvas neighbors and businesses around the locations. See if they recognize him. It's worth a shot."

I glanced back down at the file in my hand. "What do you need from me?"

"Can you look through some of the video footage we've collected? Make sure this guy isn't on camera near any of the locations?"

I nodded. "Sure."

I silently apologized to my eyes for the tedium I was about to put them through. Maybe it was time to invest in a gallon jug of eye drops. We really needed more help for a project like this, but the state had bigger fish to fry than a small-town serial arsonist. The only reason they weren't more dedicated to this case was because there weren't any casualties yet. Just our lovely close call.

Eventually that might change. But until then, we had to do the best we could with the resources we had.

Chapter Five

SETH

THIS HAD to be by far the craziest thing I'd done. And I run into burning buildings for a living. But going on a fake date just so I didn't have to deal with women who wanted to sleep with me? Something had to be wrong with me.

The door to the small townhome swung open and I couldn't stop my gaze from trailing down her body. Violet's style was definitely...weird.

So why did I like it so much?

The short-sleeved, dark purple top she wore zipped up the front, the neckline dipping low to reveal the deep valley between her breasts. A short black skirt was paired with her signature fishnets, and my eyes followed the toned curves of her legs to black come-fuck-me high-heeled boots.

I shifted uncomfortably on my feet, trying to hide my obvious reaction to her outfit.

"Ready?" Damn. I cleared my throat, that single word sounding husky even to me.

A smile lit up her face. "Not sure people will believe we're on a date if you're glowering at me the whole time."

"I glower at everyone. People annoy me."

She rolled her eyes and stepped out on the landing, pulling her door shut behind her.

Turning to the side, I waved down the sidewalk, getting in step next to her. I itched to reach out and place my hand on the small of her back, but I shoved my hand in my pocket instead. This wasn't a real date.

Once we reached the car, I opened the passenger side door and she brushed past me, her sweet floral and honey scent floating up and invading my senses. I couldn't stop myself from zeroing in on her thighs as she sat in the seat, her skirt riding up. I swallowed as I followed a path up her body, pausing at her cleavage that, at this angle, was even more pronounced. She shifted as she put her seatbelt on and I yanked my gaze away.

I really needed to pull my shit together and not ogle her every chance I had. I shut the door, making my way around to the driver's side.

"What are you doing?" I asked as I pulled the car away from the curb.

She held a cord for her phone in her hand and plugged it into my car. "Putting on decent music."

Billie Eilish began playing through the speakers. Interesting choice, although I didn't hate it.

"What was wrong with my music?"

"It's depressing."

"Depressing? It's country."

"Yeah. Some of it's okay. But mostly sad. Someone is always grieving something."

"Billie Eilish isn't much better."

"Ehh." She shrugged. "I only put her uplifting songs on my playlists. Same with Adona."

"Who else do you like?" Now I was curious. I just assumed by her dark look she would be heavily into true goth music or heavy metal.

She spit out the names of ten more artists. Some I didn't recognize, but the mix she mentioned seemed to be mostly pop and punk rock.

"What about you? Are you strictly a country boy?"

"I'll listen to just about anything." I ran my hand over my head, brushing back the long lock of hair that fell in front of my face. "Classical is probably my go-to. I enjoy listening to just the instruments."

She chuckled. "You're an enigma, Mountain Man."

I ignored the nickname and cocked a brow. "How so?"

"From the bear hug you gave me yesterday to classical music, you keep surprising me."

"I could say the same for you," I muttered with a shake of my head. From the outside, she looked dark and scary. But in reality, she smelled like sunflowers, was afraid of heights, and baked cookies.

"I like to keep people on their toes." After a few minutes of silence, during which she gently rocked her head side to side along with a song I definitely didn't recognize, she asked, "So where are we going?"

"The Dock."

"Smart move."

I smiled. It was a calculated move. I figured dinner time on a Friday evening at the town's most popular restaurant was the best guarantee news would get around quickly.

What I hadn't considered was how well-loved Violet was in town. By the time we were seated at our table, at least five people had stopped and talked to us. Some shot us knowing smirks, while a few seemed surprised to see us out together. Regardless, my plan was working.

Violet reached across the table and laid her hand on top of mine. A zap traveled up my arm and shot south. I went to pull my arm back, but her grip tightened.

"The women at the table off to your right keep staring at us and whispering to each other." She smiled. "Pretend you like me."

I stole a quick glance out of my peripheral. Violet was right, they were definitely staring. I turned my hand over and grasped hers, trying—and failing—to ignore how small and dainty her hand was compared to mine. How soft her skin was. How the simple touch was wreaking havoc on my body.

Almost absentmindedly, I brushed my thumb across the skin on the back of her hand, and when I felt her shiver under my touch, I raised my gaze to her face. She stared intently at her menu, giving away nothing else.

We sat like that, together but seemingly in our own little worlds, until the waiter appeared and Violet pulled her hand back.

After we ordered and were left alone once again, I leaned back in my chair. Conversation wasn't something I was good at. But it wasn't like this was the first time I'd been on a date.

Fake date, I reminded myself.

When was the last time I'd done this? Months? Before I'd moved here for sure. But then, that was with Lucy, and we'd been together for years before things ended right before I moved. So that was not really a first date situation.

"Did you read the comments?"

I raised a brow. "What?"

"That video of you bringing me down the ladder. Did you read the comments?"

I scoffed and rolled my eyes. "Those women were shameless."

She chuckled. "Some of them were pretty funny."

"It's a total double standard, you know. If I was a woman, that would have never happened."

"Oh, totally." A smirk pulled at her lips. "But most single guys would like the attention."

"And you think I'm like most single guys?"

She shook her head. "No. I definitely do not."

I had to smirk at the way she said it. And of course she caught it.

"Is that a smile?"

I schooled my features. "Don't get used to it."

As she smirked back, her tiny nose ring glinted, catching my eye. "How many piercings do you have?"

"Twelve."

Most of them looked to be in her ears, but that didn't stop me from wondering where the ones I couldn't see were. My gaze traveled down to the small rose covered in spiderwebs on her right wrist.

"Tattoos?"

"Three," she said before adding, "but I want a few more."

And now I was back to thinking about the places on her body that weren't currently visible.

"I had a place I liked in Asheville. Shame there aren't any shops here in town."

I blinked and forced my gaze back to her face. "The drive to Asheville isn't far."

"I know."

"Is that where you're from?"

She shook her head. "No, I grew up in New York. Went to college at Western Carolina. Lived in Asheville post-graduation for three years before moving here. What about you?"

I debated how much I wanted to tell her. Typically I offered the least possible amount, if anything, of personal information. So what was it about this woman that made me want to answer her questions? Not that it mattered, because she didn't even give me the chance to reply before she jumped in with a different question.

"Do you have other tattoos, besides the one on your right shoulder?"

Once again she surprised me, detouring from what I expected. And why did I like it so much that she noticed my tattoo? "Yeah. One on my calf and another on my back."

"I'm surprised Mr. Serious has tattoos." The corner of her lips lifted into a smirk.

I didn't see the connection, so I just shrugged. I also didn't see myself as super serious. I just didn't like people. Or, rather, I found them exhausting.

After a moment of silence she asked, "Where are you from?"

"Charlotte."

"Why'd you move here?"

I let out a long sigh. Apparently our detour was over. How did I answer this? Sticking to the most basic of truths seemed like the best course. "I decided I wasn't cut out for life in a busy city. A house in the mountains and small-town life is more my style. Although now I'm second-guessing if I'm actually going to get more peace and quiet here."

She shrugged. "Eventually. The town will invariably move on to something else and the whole *'save a ladder, climb a firefighter'* thing will be long forgotten."

I rolled my eyes at the reminder of the ridiculous caption. "Does it not bother you?"

"The video?"

"Yeah."

"Not really." She chuckled awkwardly. "But I don't let much bother me."

One of the siblings of the family that owns The Dock stepped up to our table with our food, placing it down in front of us. "Seriously, first Logan and now Seth? I really need to stop by the firehouse more often. They seem to be dropping like flies," she directed at Violet with a wink.

I rolled my eyes. She was ridiculous. Anytime we came in here, she would shamelessly flirt with any or all of us. I couldn't remember what her name was, I only remembered her as the flirty one with different colored hair that changed every few months. She turned her gaze on me, and I sighed.

"You guys should make T-shirts with that 'climb a firefighter' caption, by the way. I bet every woman in town would buy one."

I shook my head. "No." We were definitely not making fucking T-shirts. Jesus.

"Just saying." She shrugged. "Enjoy." She directed that single word at Violet before shooting her a wink and walking away.

"She's my favorite." Violet's eyes twinkled with mischief. "Makes me laugh every time."

"Somehow that doesn't surprise me."

While Violet and I ate our food, we continued to chat between bites. And by the time the check came, I realized something.

I actually enjoyed having dinner with her.

Chapter Six

VIOLET

DINNER WITH SETH was surprisingly not bad. I'd worried he would be hard to talk to. But other than a handful of times when silence passed between us, it wasn't an issue. It wasn't even awkward silence, just felt like natural pauses in the conversation while we ate.

He held the door to The Dock open, letting me exit first. Brushing past him, I got the same whiff of leather with a hint of wood that I had gotten earlier in the evening. It suited the Mountain Man.

I came to a halt outside as I narrowed my eyes at my ex approaching from the parking lot. Did he know I was here? He grew up in this town, so I wouldn't be surprised if someone told him I was on a date. It was what I'd hoped would happen to cement what I'd texted him. I didn't think he'd show up though.

"You okay?" Seth asked.

"Really, Violet?" James scoffed. "The firefighter who saved you? Is that why you two looked so *friendly*?" The way he said friendly didn't match what the word meant. "Because you're banging him?"

Seth growled and took a step forward, but I grabbed him by the hand and squeezed. This wasn't his battle to fight, and I wouldn't give this asshole any more of our time.

"At least I waited until we were broken up to *bang* someone else. Can't say the same for you, unfortunately." Showing up at his apartment earlier than I was supposed to and catching him with Evelyn—the young twenty-year-old wearing nothing but a towel and a smirk—was still etched in my brain. I looked up at Seth. "Come on babe, let's go."

He stared at me for a beat before nodding and placing his hand on my lower back, ushering me forward.

As we passed James, Seth slowed. "Don't ever talk to her like that again."

He didn't even need to outline the consequences a repeat performance would result in. Between how much taller Seth was compared to James, and the way he said the words, it was intimidating enough.

Once in the car, I forced my shoulders to relax. Seth climbed in the driver's seat and turned to me. "You dated that tool?"

"Try not to remind me." It definitely wasn't the best decision I'd ever made. But he was sweet when we'd first started dating last fall. As time went on, though, I realized how self-centered and unreliable he could be. Apparently untrustworthy too.

"Let me know if he bothers you again. I can have a chat with him if you want me to."

I smiled over at the big burly man who was nothing like I'd imagined him to be. "Thanks."

Seth nodded and started the car. "Hopefully people seeing us around town together will help relay the message to fuck off."

I angled my head to the side. "Is that your way of asking me out again?"

He scoffed. "Well, people aren't going to believe we're really dating if we're only seen together once. If we're really going to sell it, we have to go out again. Right?"

I laughed at the absurdity of this conversation. And to think, every time I'd read a fake dating romance, I never once thought it was realistic. Now, here I was, living one.

"Or not," he added.

Heavens. The dejection in his voice was too much. I would have never guessed that beneath the surface, Mountain Man had so many layers.

"You're right. We should definitely do this again."

If I was being honest, he wasn't horrible to be around. I'd actually enjoyed our "date." And if *fake* dating him kept James away from me, then why not? I just needed to make sure we were both on the same page.

"I'm not ready to *actually* date again, but this way I can show James I've moved on."

This would benefit both of us in the long run. I just had to ignore the flutter that had raced up my arm and down my spine as he'd brushed his thumb across the back of my hand at the table. Or the way I felt protected when his hand landed on my lower back. And how he stood up for me, growling at my ex.

That was all. Easy peasy.

Chapter Seven

SETH

Monday 9:12 a.m.

Me: How does lunch sound?

Violet: Today?

Me: Yeah, if you're free.

Me: I'm on night shifts for the next 3 nights.

Violet: Okay. That should be fine. Where do you want to meet?

Me: I'll pick you up. At work?

Violet: Yeah. Noon?

Me: Perfect.

Violet: Will you bring me flowers this time?

Me: Probably not.

Violet: Aren't you supposed to be wooing me?

Me: ...

Violet: You're glaring at the phone, aren't you?

Me: Yes.

Violet: Aww look how well we know each other already.

Me: See you at noon, Violet.

Violet: Sigh. You're no fun.

Chapter Eight

SETH

I OPENED the door to the police station and glanced over at Violet who stood talking to the desk sergeant. I waited, not wanting to interrupt, and after a moment she looked my way.

She turned and moved toward me, and a smile tugged at my lips as I read her T-shirt: *School sucks. Start a band.*

I shook my head and held the door so she could exit in front of me. I'd debated texting her all weekend. I had no idea what I was supposed to do. Not only had it been more than two years since I started dating someone, this also wasn't actual dating.

But I couldn't stop thinking about that asshole ex of hers. I wanted to make sure he stayed away from her. And if spending a little bit of time with her solved both of our problems, I didn't see that as the worst thing that could happen. Ultimately, that was what led to me finally texting her this morning.

"Anywhere specific you'd like to go?" I asked her, stopping outside on the sidewalk.

"The diner's always good."

"Perfect."

We walked to my car parked down the street and I held the passenger door open for her. I tried not to stare at her legs, clad in fishnets and cutoff denim shorts, as she climbed into the car. And I was as unsuccessful this time as I was last time. Something about those damn fishnets kept pulling me in. I chuckled at the fact that she hooked her phone back up to my car to play her own music, just like she did on Friday, as I drove toward the diner.

"You guys still working the arson case?" I hadn't heard an update, but then again I'd been off since Friday, so if there was, I wouldn't know.

"Yup." She let out a long sigh. "We're basically starting over. I'm going through all the video footage we've collected since January looking for anything we've missed. Or anyone that seems out of place."

"So you're not looking at the Taylor kid anymore?"

She shrugged. "We can't touch him until we solve the fires he has alibis for. It's basically one of three scenarios. One, he didn't start any of the fires. Two, he's working with someone. Or three, he's responsible for all but two fires. But until we figure out who set those two, or until the guy messes up, there's not much we can do."

"Could be a woman."

"Not likely. Statistics say it's probably a man. But who knows? I'm personally not ruling anyone out at this point."

"We had one in Charlotte."

"One?" Her brows pulled together.

"A woman arsonist."

"Huh." She stared at me. "Is there an interesting story that goes with that tidbit?"

I shrugged. "Abusive husband. She decided burning the house down with both of them inside was better than living."

Why the hell was I even talking about this? Not really date material.

Fake date. I reminded myself.

"Ouch. Did either survive?"

"He didn't. She did, but ended up being convicted of manslaughter and arson."

I still thought about that woman from time to time. The way she cried in relief when her husband was pronounced dead at the scene.

"You guys probably saw a lot of crazy stuff being in a city."

"Once got called to a car that got wedged between two buildings. It's hard enough having to cut someone out, but having two large unmovable objects on either side made it near impossible."

"I can imagine."

I pulled into a parking space and turned off the engine. Our conversation waned as we made our way to the building, but I instinctively held the door to the diner open and ushered her inside, resting my hand on her lower back. She grabbed my hand, and I stiffened, thinking I'd overstepped. She twined our fingers together, and when I looked down at her, her wide smile made me relax as we waited for the hostess to return.

Luckily there wasn't a wait and we followed the hostess to an empty table. I wasn't sure if anyone would notice, or care, but holding her hand definitely had date written all over it.

"See, I told you," a feminine voice said from a nearby table.

Even though the words registered as I took my seat, I didn't think they were talking to or about me. Until recently, people around Half Moon Lake had left me alone. For some reason, that damn video made people think I was approachable. I didn't understand it, nor did I like it.

Violet smiled and waved over my shoulder. I followed her gaze and bit back a groan. Logan and his girlfriend Izzy sat in a booth with Logan's twin daughters. Shouldn't they be in school? It was almost the middle of August. Maybe school hadn't started back yet?

I tipped my chin at Logan and turned back to Violet.

"Do you want to go say hi?" she asked.

I raised a brow. Was she serious? Why did she think I wanted to go say hi? I worked with him and would see him later that night. I didn't see a reason to interrupt our meals by chatting.

The corners of her lips twitched. "Never mind. Forget I asked that."

I went back to looking over the menu, and when the waitress came over a few minutes later, we placed our orders.

Logan's daughters skipped past the table and Izzy slowed down to pause next to us, Logan right behind her. Great. Were they planning to stand here and talk to us?

"You two are dating now, right?" Izzy looked from me to Violet. "Logan doesn't believe it."

"Yes," I blurted out and narrowed my eyes at Logan. After our conversation last week, I'd wondered if the guys would believe we were really dating. "We are."

Logan's lips lifted into a smirk. "Come on, sweetheart. Let them get back to their *date*."

Fucker.

The way he emphasized the last word made it obvious he still wasn't buying it. And why did I even care? I didn't need the guys to believe it, just the rest of this crazy-ass town.

Finally, we were alone again.

"You didn't tell the guys we're faking?"

I shook my head. "No."

"Why?"

I had no clue. Probably because I wasn't sure any of them understood my issue with the attention. "I figured it was on a need-to-know basis, and none of them needed to know."

She chuckled. "Anyone ever tell you you're strange?"

I raised one brow at her. Now wasn't that calling the kettle black. "Could say the same for you."

Her shoulders lifted and fell in a shrug. "Only until they get to know me."

I was finding her even more strange—or maybe surprising was the right word—since the fire the prior week. Outwardly, she portrayed dark and gloomy. But in reality, she wasn't either.

The minutes ticked by as we waited for our food, silence surrounding us. I shifted uncomfortably, finally relaxing when she began talking about a new band she'd found on TikTok.

I ignored the looks we were getting from people around us. I had to let them contemplate what was going on between us. For this to really work, small-town gossip had to do its thing.

Once our food was delivered, Violet filled the space between bites with small talk. She was good at this, and didn't seem to mind that I wasn't. I found out she was twenty-seven—a little more than a year younger than me—an only child, and that she liked the weather here better than in New York.

"What about you?"

"Me?"

"Yeah. Tell me something about you. Do you have family in Charlotte?"

I grunted and nodded. When she continued to stare at me expectantly, I shifted uncomfortably. "My parents live in the city. My brother lives in the suburbs with his wife and daughter. She's six."

We continued to chat as we ate—actually, it was more her leading the conversation and asking pointed questions. But again, she didn't seem to mind.

By the time we paid the check and made our way back to the car, I didn't hate the idea of having to do this again. I wasn't sure if being seen together twice was enough for the town to believe we were dating. We probably should go out one more time just in case.

Would she agree to that?

Chapter Nine

VIOLET

SETH ACTED like he wanted to say something else when he dropped me back off. He was so awkward, it was actually kind of cute. I didn't want to push him. It was obvious conversation didn't come easy to him. Somehow I didn't see the reclusive, quiet, burly man as much of a dater.

I sat back down at my desk and pulled up the footage I'd been looking through before I left for lunch. It was from the bakery that faced the road to the old BBQ joint. Dylan's hope was that we would see who drove or walked in or out from Main Street. Patrols were out, working on canvasing the homes further up the road to see if we could gather any ring camera footage as well. He didn't want to rule anyone out, and if I saw something even remotely suspicious, he wanted me to bring it to his attention.

Our original suspect's godfather hadn't been on any footage near any of the fires so far. But whoever it was had been vigilant about not being seen by anyone, so none of us were surprised. The fire at the BBQ place didn't match the others under investigation. They were started in the very early morning hours, before the sun came up and businesses were open. Not this one. This one was started in the late afternoon. It also didn't have the same burn patterns or broken window that the others did. All that added up to the reason the lead arson investigator suggested we focus on this one. If it was our arsonist, and it was an unplanned fire, they would have been more likely to mess up, leaving vital clues behind.

I had started my day early, and after watching another hour of footage, I was almost ready to call it a day. There was only so much my eyes could take. But then I startled, sitting up straight and abruptly pressing the button to pause the video as I stared at a familiar face glancing back across the street as they turned to walk down the road.

What the hell was he doing there? I pushed play again and watched intently as James continued down the street toward the BBQ place. He glanced back once more, his actions more than a little suspicious.

We were still together at that point. He knew I had been helping the investigators. Why didn't he tell me he was there right before the fire started? Maybe he saw something.

Only one way I was going to find out. I pulled out my phone and shot off a text.

> Me: Can you meet? I need to talk to you.

> Asshole: Did you come to your senses and realize you made a mistake?

I rolled my eyes. The mistake was ever dating him. But you get more bees with honey than vinegar, right?

Me: I just need to talk. It's important.

Asshole: Fine. Coffee shop?

Me: Perfect.

The coffee shop was on the far side of town from the police station, but just across the street from the auto shop where James worked. It was extremely convenient for him, not so much for me. Nevertheless, it had been our usual meetup on weekdays when we were both at work. Shocker, I know.

I grabbed my bag and headed out of my office, pausing in the hallway. Should I let Dylan know? He probably wouldn't let me go alone. James was harmless, I knew that, but Dylan didn't. He was trained to think everyone was a threat.

Was this really a situation where I would need protection? We were meeting in a busy public place. And I just wanted to see why James was even on the video. He could have parked his car on that street and gone to the bakery. But on a Friday afternoon? That just didn't track for him.

I walked quickly out of the station and turned right, heading down Main Street. It wasn't that far, maybe only fifteen or twenty minutes, and on a nice day I enjoyed the walk. But the walk over also brought back memories of too many times we'd met there when it was raining or cold. Definitely more of an inconvenience for me, and there were closer places to my job we could have met. Just one more example of things being all about him.

Well, not any more. Fake relationship or not, whatever I had now was better than anything I'd had with James.

Inside the small space, I glanced around. James was at a table in the far corner. Once I reached him, I pulled out the chair across from him and sat down.

"You've ignored me for days and now you desperately need to talk?"

I sighed. It wasn't my fault he couldn't take a hint. "It's work-related. About the fire back in May."

57

All the color drained from his face, and he looked around the shop and then back down at the table in front of us. "What about it?"

Geesh. Why was he acting so weird?

"Why didn't you tell me you were in the area around the time of the fire?"

He whipped his gaze up and his eyes widened. "What?"

Did I want to lay all my cards on the table? If I wanted his help, I had no choice. "I'm going through a bunch of video footage and saw you walking up the street minutes before the call came in."

He stared at me but didn't say anything.

I shifted slightly in my seat, starting to feel a tad uncomfortable. "You knew I was brought in to help, so I'm confused why you didn't tell me. Did you see anything?"

He shook his head and looked away, refusing to meet my gaze again. He was almost acting paranoid, on the verge of suspicious. Suddenly, I felt nervous that I came by myself. But I was in a public place, and there were plenty of people in here, so I took a deep breath and asked the question that came to mind.

"It wasn't you, was it?" I muttered, instantly regretting it. It wasn't like he would admit it or anything.

His gaze met mine again and he narrowed his eyes. "No, of course not." Then he sighed, dropping his head and fiddled with the napkin on the table.

"Then why are you acting so weird?"

He leaned forward, placing his forearms on the table. "I was meeting Evelyn," he finally whispered.

My stomach turned in the worst way. "But—" That was a month before I showed up at his apartment and caught him with her. "You said—"

I didn't need to finish that sentence. Obviously, he'd lied when he said it was a one-time thing. A fucking month. Bile rose in my throat. He was sleeping with both of us for a month? Oh God. Or longer?

I pulled my shoulders back and schooled my features. I wasn't going to give him the satisfaction of getting a reaction out of me. Frankly, catching him cheating was the best thing that could have happened to me. It showed me who he really was.

"Whatever." I waved my hand. "I just need to know if you saw anything. Anyone or anything suspicious?"

"No." He shook his head. "Didn't see anyone except a bunch of teenagers goofing off."

"Teenagers?"

"Yeah. We were in the car, um...talking." He sat back in his chair and crossed his arms, and I fought the urge to vomit at what he wasn't saying. "A bunch of teenage boys walked by. They were the only people I saw come up or down the road."

I made a mental note to look at the footage again and let Dylan know. If we could find the teenagers, maybe they could tell us something helpful.

"Okay. Thanks." I pushed my chair back and stood up.

"Violet—"

I held up my hand, cutting off whatever he was going to say. "James, I've moved on, and there's absolutely no chance in hell I would consider getting back together with you. So please stop texting me."

With that, I turned and walked away.

Good thing I didn't have to go back to the station because there was no way I could focus after what I'd just found out. My body vibrated with anger and I felt like I was on the brink of fighting tears. I needed a minute to process and collect myself.

Once I was far enough down Main Street, I pulled out my phone and opened my text thread with Hattie.

> Me: Please tell me you're at work.

Her family owned The Dock and she took care of the accounting side of things, so I was praying she was there today.

> Hattie: Yeah, I'm here.

> Me: I'm coming over. Might need a drink.

> Hattie: Uh oh. What did asshole James do now?

I smiled. My nicknaming habit seemed to be rubbing off on her.

> Me: He was cheating on me for at least a month. Probably more.

> Hattie: I'll have a shot ready for you when you get here.

> Me: Thanks.

One drink, and then I would head home and lose myself in a pint of Ben and Jerry's.

The Dock was super close, which was good. Less time to stew on it all. Or less time to plan a murder and decide which endangered shrubs to bury the body under.

Once I stepped through the door, I spotted Hattie standing with Savannah behind the bar and made my way toward them. Climbing up on a stool, I took the shot from Hattie and threw it back.

"Starting happy hour with shots?" Savannah smirked. "My kind of girl."

"Well, when you find out your ex was cheating on you for more than a month, it requires shots."

"Oh shit," Savannah said before giving a slight shrug of her shoulders. "But you're dating that hot as fuck firefighter now. Definitely leveled-up."

I met Hattie's gaze, and her lips twitched. "She has a point."

I tried not to react. She knew I wasn't really dating Seth. Telling her all about it at breakfast after Seth asked me to fake date him was a no-brainer. I couldn't keep something like that from one of my close friends.

"Best thing you can do is show him you've moved on, and with someone a hell of a lot better than him."

Right. That was my plan. That didn't mean Seth wanted to continue to pretend to date me. But he was the one who started this crazy idea, after all, so maybe I could get him to agree to continue it.

Chapter Ten

SETH

I STUDIED the cards in my hand, ignoring the looks aimed my way by the guys sitting at the table with me. This was the first time we'd sat down since starting our shift. Everything was done that needed to be done and now we were just killing time.

"Are you really dating Violet?" Logan asked.

And there it was. I could tell he'd wanted to say something since we sat down ten minutes earlier.

I looked across the table at him, keeping my features schooled in a neutral expression, waiting to see where he was taking this. He leaned back and crossed his arms over his chest. I wasn't sure what he wanted me to say. Admit that I'd asked Violet to go out with me so the women in this town would leave me alone? The guys would give me crap for weeks. I'd likely never hear the end of it.

"You just saw us at lunch earlier." I glanced back down at my cards, keeping my voice even as I pulled one from my hand and threw it on the discard pile.

"Yeah, but—"

His attention diverted up to the ceiling as the red lights surrounding the PA speaker illuminated. We stood, and the alarms blared loudly as we made our way down to the bay.

Damn. Reports of a brush fire. Depending on where, it could easily move into the forest. I was still getting familiar with all the areas of Half Moon Lake, and from the information dispatch was relaying, I couldn't pinpoint exactly where the fire was.

"We might need more water. Ricktor," Owen called over to Adam, "you and Davis, bring the tanker. Everyone else with Murray."

Owen jogged to the utility truck and headed out. Logan, Jay, and Zack climbed up into the engine truck as Adam and I headed to the water tender truck.

If this turned into a wildfire—or worse, a fully involved forest fire—we would definitely need more water than the engine could carry. Hell, depending on how bad things got, we might be calling in surrounding stations to assist too.

Once on scene, Owen began dishing out commands. Setting up supply lines from the engine and connecting the tanker to the intake of the engine's pump was a priority, allowing for a continuous water supply.

This was the second one of these we'd seen in the last week. Between the late summer heat and limited rain lately, everything was dry. And even though we were currently under a burn ban, it didn't mean people listened. This one was likely caused by a lightning strike, a result of a nasty storm that had just come through. It wasn't huge, and luckily we were far enough away from the tree line that stopping it from spreading wasn't an unrealistic goal.

But even once we put it out in this area, we'd need to keep an eye on it for reignition.

We desperately needed some rain.

We all got to work, and when two more trucks from other stations showed up to assist, Owen told us all to take a quick break. We'd start a rotation now with each crew taking a break while the rest worked the fire.

I tossed fresh bottles of water to everyone. Staying hydrated was paramount. We would be useless if one of us passed out from dehydration. And with all of us running around in full gear, it was a real concern. Adrenaline was always high in these situations, and the mission forefront in our minds; it was easier than you'd think to forget something as simple as drinking water.

Thankfully, the sun had set not long ago. If the temperatures started to drop and humidity levels rose, this fire would be easier to control and extinguish.

Either way, I had a feeling tonight was going to be a long one.

Chapter Eleven

VIOLET

TUESDAY 5:22 P.M.

Mountain Man: I think we should go out again.

Me: You really need to work on your delivery.

Mountain Man: ...

Me: Sigh.

Mountain Man: People were staring at me at the grocery store today.

Me: Are they not allowed to look at you?

Mountain Man: Yeah, but then the cashier was super chatty.

Me: *eyeroll emoji*

Me: Maybe she was just being friendly.

Mountain Man: One more date. Just to make sure.

Me: And then what?

Mountain Man: What do you mean?

Me: I have a better proposal. For both of us. Let's say 2-3 months. We go out in public once or twice a week and pretend we're dating until November. It will guarantee all the women in town have completely moved on, and it'll make my ex regret ever cheating on me. Win win.

Mountain Man: Deal.

Me: That was quick. You sure you don't want to think about it?

Mountain Man: Why?

Me: Just to be sure.

Mountain Man: No, I'm good.

Me. Okie Dokey.

Me: Do you work this Saturday?

Mountain Man: No.

Me: A bunch of us are going out for Savannah's birthday.

Mountain Man: Who?

OUT OF THE FIRE

Me: Savannah Williams? Youngest Williams sibling?

Mountain Man: ...

Me: Sigh. Owners of The Dock? She's the one who brought our food the other night? Blue and purple hair?

Mountain Man: Okay.

Me: Anyway, it's probably not your scene. You know, fun and social. But if you want to come with me, you can. Hattie's bringing Dylan.

Me: Or we can plan lunch or dinner a different day.

Mountain Man: Okay.

Me: Man of many words

I sat my phone down and picked up the rose quartz necklace I was working on before Seth had texted. Once I finished that, I began making a pair of earrings to go with the necklace. The set was for an order placed through my online store, but I liked how it turned out so much, I decided to make a second pair for me.

Rose quartz was often used to help release negativity, anger, and resentment. It would probably be good for me. I wore my citrine necklace almost all the time, and I thought it worked pretty well to evoke joy and positivity. Adding the rose quartz could help with emotional healing. Well, at least it couldn't hurt, right?

Although it was also thought to attract new love, which was not something I was looking for. Yet another reason the idea of fake dating Seth was enticing. I could show James I'd moved on and have someone to go do things with without actually dating.

Speaking of the big burly man who still hadn't texted back. By now he was probably on shift.

Me: So... okay you'll come Saturday night? Or okay you want to plan something else?

Mountain Man: The first one.

Me: You really don't like words, do you?

Mountain Man: I don't like unnecessary words. I just got to the station. I can text later.

I smiled. Technically, he didn't need to text me at all. But for some reason I liked the idea that he might.

I made myself a late dinner and went back to making some jewelry. I'd been doing it since I was a teenager and I'd always found the process therapeutic.

Thoughts of my mom drifted into my head, and I picked up my phone. It had been too long since I'd talked to my parents.

"Hey, chickadee," my mom said with her usual zest.

I smiled at the nickname she still called me. "Hi, Ma."

"We were just talking about you."

The last two times she'd called, I couldn't talk because I was at work, but we'd texted instead. I didn't get the sense there was anything important she was calling about. And she would have told me to call her back if it were urgent.

"Oh?" I popped in one earbud and sat my phone back down on the table, going back to twisting the metal around the crystal I was working on.

"We know it's still a few months away, but what do you think about us coming down there for Thanksgiving this year?"

"Really?"

"Yeah. Dad and I both have time off that week, so we figured it would be nice to get away for a few days."

"I love that idea."

"Good." Her voice sounded further away as she relayed my response to my father.

I leaned forward and sifted through my box of supplies, attempting to locate an O-ring for the pendant in my hand.

"What are you doing?" she asked.

"Making some jewelry."

"Ahh. I miss those days when you would sit in the middle of the floor, making jewelry for hours."

I chuckled. "Except it was hard to get my attention."

"Oh yeah. When you were locked in, a bomb could go off and you'd be totally unfazed."

She wasn't wrong. I was like that at a crime scene sometimes too. Probably part of the reason I hadn't realized the fire had rekindled at the farmhouse last week.

We talked a bit more, and I felt better that I'd finally gotten to talk to her. I was excited for them to come visit at Thanksgiving. It was the perfect amount of time to catch up without feeling like they were smothering me.

She passed the phone over to my dad. He almost immediately asked me if I was keeping up on my oil changes and about the faucet that dripped in the kitchen that I had told him about a few weeks ago. I had to shake my head at him, but secretly I loved that he worried about me. After confirming I had recently taken care of both of those things, we talked for another twenty minutes about the latest *NCIS* episode he had just watched before saying goodnight and hanging up.

By the time I climbed into my bed later that night, Seth still hadn't texted back. I opted not to dwell on that fact. For one, his job could be demanding, and if he wasn't on a call, he might be resting before the next alarm sounded. Two, we weren't really dating. The expectations were different.

Plus, I wasn't the type of person who dwelled on negativity. Even with my career choice, I tried not to. Him not replying to me was not a reflection of who I was.

I could, however, admit James had been a shitty boyfriend. Cheating aside, I'd never felt that I could truly depend on him. He constantly said he would do things and rarely followed through.

Next time I threw myself into a relationship, I wouldn't settle. I deserved better, and I had to believe the kind of guy who understood that was out there. He'd find his way into my life when the time was right for both of us.

SETH

I looked at the time and wondered if it was too late to text Violet. I would have done it earlier, but almost as soon as my shift started, we were pulled out on back-to-back calls. I pulled up our text thread and typed out a quick message.

> Me: Sorry. Been busy with calls. I'm good with Saturday, just let me know the details.

A text notification from my brother came through and I switched over to my thread with him.

> Mason: You busy?

> Me: On shift, but not really. What's up?

> Mason: Shelby's mad at me again.

> Mason: I just don't know what to do.

> Mason: She seems to really be struggling going back to work full time. But she gets upset at me when I suggest ways to make it better.

> Me: You guys will figure it out. You always do.

My brother and Shelby had been together since I was like twelve or thirteen. Got married ten years ago at the end of my senior year in high school. They had always been perfect together. The type of relationship I thought I was going to have with Lucy, until that completely crumbled into a million pieces. But this last year was the first time they'd struggled.

> Mason: I don't know, man. Hopefully you're right.

> Mason: How's things going there? Women still knocking down your door?

> Me: No. I fixed that.

> Mason: Oh?

I smirked. He would probably laugh and give me shit but I didn't care. We'd always been close and I rarely hid anything from him.

> Me: The town thinks I'm dating someone now.

> Mason: Thinks?

> Me: Yeah, we're pretending.

> Mason: I'm going to need the full story at some point. That seems so unlike you.

> Me: I'll call you tomorrow morning when I get off shift.

> Mason: Ok. Stay safe tonight.

> Me: Will do.

Chapter Twelve

VIOLET

I'D SPENT the day before going through ring camera footage Dylan and his partner, Aiden, had gathered from the street where the BBQ place was, with no luck spotting the teenagers James had mentioned. I was staring down another day of the same with two more to view before heading home for the day.

"You're going to hate me."

I spun my chair to see Dylan standing in the doorway of my office. He held a small, opaque blue bag in his hand.

I angled my head. "What is it?"

He stepped forward and placed the bag on the corner of my desk. "The poop bandit struck again."

I scrunched my nose at the offending parcel. "Please tell me that's not what I think it is."

"I wish I could."

"And what is it you think I'm going to do with that?"

"Test the DNA."

My eyes widened. "You're not serious?"

The look of apology he sent me did nothing to help the *situation*. I did not get paid enough for this crap. Pun intended.

"We've had numerous complaints about this for months—"

"Yeah, because some people have entirely too much time on their hands."

"But if we can track down who's doing it, put a little fear of repercussions into them, hopefully they'll get their, ummm...shit together and clean up after their pet. Captain's frustrated, too. Filing all these reports every time someone complains is using unnecessary manpower." He sighed. "Plus, Captain's sister-in-law is on the HOA board and asked him to help them out with this first case. The neighborhood HOA just passed a rule that requires DNA testing of all the dogs in the community. They'll set up and register with one of those companies that does dog waste enforcement."

I rolled my eyes. I could sympathize with not wanting to tell your wife's sister no, but he wasn't the one who had to test this shit. Literally. They really needed to pay me more.

"Fine," I huffed.

"I'll make it up to you." He chuckled darkly, and I legitimately worried about what he was thinking. "I'll have one of the guys pull James over for something stupid."

I shook my head. "He isn't worth it." Although the idea did sound somewhat enticing.

He tipped his head to my computer screen. "Focus on the ring camera footage. The dog shit can wait."

"I would prefer to get that out of the way so it's not sitting in my office all day."

"Fair enough." He turned to leave the office, then glanced back over his shoulder. "Send me the results and let me know if you get anything off the footage."

I stared at the bag on my desk after Dylan left my office and sighed. I still couldn't believe I had to do this.

The literal crap that had landed on my desk done, I turned my focus back to the videos. After watching a few hours of footage, I paused the tape and jumped up, heading out to find Dylan.

"I got them," I announced excitedly as I approached his desk.

"The teenagers?"

"Yes. One of the cameras caught them running across the street a few houses up the street from the fire."

He stood. "Show me."

I turned and headed back toward my office, excited to have caught another break. Hopefully we could identify at least one of these kids and they could give us a new lead.

Chapter Thirteen

SETH

I SHIFTED the foil-covered pot in my right arm. Was this dumb? The idea of cut flowers had never sat well with me. You give someone something that dies in a couple of days. It was not only a waste of money, but kind of a dumb gesture. Well, to me, at least.

Ever since I was a teenager, I would give my mom potted plants for special occasions, and then I started doing that for my ex. Lucy never really appreciated it, so I stopped, but my mom loved having plants around the house and flowers in the gardens outside.

I wanted to do something for Violet that showed my appreciation for agreeing to my ludicrous plan in the first place. Now, standing outside her house, I cringed, wondering if I hadn't thought this through very well. Or maybe overthought it. What if Violet liked a vase full of flowers?

Shit. I had no idea what Violet liked.

I rang the doorbell and stepped back. We hadn't talked since Wednesday morning, and that was just her response to my text from the night before to give me the details for tonight. She'd wanted to meet me at Mamacitas, but I'd convinced her to let me pick her up. That way, if she wanted to have a few drinks with her friends, she didn't have to worry about driving home.

The door swung open and her gaze immediately traveled down to the African Violet in my hands. It was a fairly low-maintenance plant, and since they shared a name, I thought it was the perfect choice.

She smiled brightly. "Is that for me?"

I nodded. At least she didn't seem to hate it. "Yeah."

She stepped back, opening the door wider. "Come on in. I have the perfect place to put it."

She turned and I followed her through the house to the kitchen, failing to stop my gaze from drifting down to the swell of her ass. Suddenly she spun back to me and I almost collided right into her, making it obvious I was distracted.

A slight pink crept up her neck and into her face as she reached out, taking the pot from my hands. "African Violets need indirect light, so I think my hutch right here would work well. The light from the sliding glass door will be enough."

My shoulders finally relaxed. Not only did she not think the gesture was stupid, but she was familiar with the plant.

While she got the plant situated, I took a minute to take in her kitchen. It was bright and airy. Neat. Pops of vibrant blues and purples. Again, the complete opposite of the way she looked. Tonight the long sleeves of her black dress matched the fishnets she wore on her legs.

"You know I was only kidding when I asked if you were finally going to bring me flowers." She turned back to face me. "I think you're the first guy to ever give me a potted plant."

I shifted on my feet, not exactly sure what to say to that. It wasn't like it surprised me. I knew most guys brought a bouquet of flowers. That just wasn't me.

"I don't do flowers."

Her brows pulled together before she chuckled. "Okay then. No flowers, only plants. Good thing I have a green thumb."

My gaze traveled over her shoulder, landing on three hanging plants suspended from the ceiling. I nodded and a grunt of approval left my lips. "Ready to go?" I asked a second later.

"Yep." She moved toward me, pausing as she brushed past and looked up at me. "Thank you."

I held her gaze and swallowed thickly. The dark makeup that lined her honey-colored eyes and the dark lipstick that made her plump lips stand out shouldn't have been so appealing. Neither should the see-through black material that covered her arms and most of her chest, showing off the swell of her breasts.

I pulled my gaze away and nodded. The last thing she needed was me making this awkward by staring at her again. She continued past me, and I caught the brief scent of honey and flowers, reminding me again of sunflowers.

I took a deep breath and followed behind her, trying to tamp down my frustration. This was never going to work if I kept noticing every little thing about her. Her amazing scent, the way her skin felt under my touch, or how her smile made her eyes light up. I needed to learn to ignore it all.

Once in the car, I reached out and stopped her from plugging her phone in. "I started you a playlist."

She stared at me before looking down at my phone plugged into the center console. "You made me a playlist," she whispered so softly I wasn't sure I heard her correctly.

I shrugged. I didn't want her to get the wrong impression, although now I worried it might come off weird. I liked a variety of music, and typically wore earbuds and listened to music whenever I worked out or went for a run. As songs I thought she might like came up on my playlist, I'd started adding them to a new playlist.

"It's just some songs I thought you'd like. You can plug yours in if you want, though."

She stared at me with parted lips for a beat and then shook her head, sitting back in her seat. "No. I want to listen to it."

Silence settled between us, the music filling the space perfectly as I drove the short drive to the Mexican restaurant.

"Not bad," she said as I parked the car.

I raised a brow at her.

"The playlist," she clarified. "I recognized a few of the songs, but there were a couple I liked but couldn't place."

Turning off the engine, I nodded and climbed out of the car, meeting her at the passenger door just as she closed it behind her. I held the door to the restaurant open and waved for her to go in front of me. We weaved through the crowded place to a long table set up against the back wall.

I tipped my head toward Dylan. Other than Violet, he was the only other person I was actually familiar with. I didn't even see the birthday girl anywhere. I slightly recognized the brunette Dylan had his arm around and Violet was currently chatting with.

Violet looked up at me. "You know Dylan, but have you met Hattie?"

When I shook my head, she introduced us and then Hattie took over introducing both of us to other people at the table. I gathered that Violet didn't know a lot of these people either. We sat down and I placed my arm along the back of her chair.

Savannah appeared at the end of the table. Who knew where she'd been for the last ten minutes. "Who wants a shot?" She grabbed one from the tray as the waitress started to make her way around the table, passing them out.

Violet took one, but I shook my head when the waitress asked. I would probably have a beer, maybe two. I'd promised Violet I would be the designated driver so she didn't have to worry about it, and I wasn't a big fan of shots anyway.

Multiple conversations were happening around the table as the waitress did another round, taking drink and food orders for those who were ready. I sat quietly as Violet talked nonstop with Hattie, trying my best to tune into her talking and filter out all the other noise.

After the waitress delivered everyone's drinks, Violet shifted close to me, leaning on my chair, her hand brushing the outside of my thigh. "Sorry, is this too much for you?"

My instinct was to say yes. For so many reasons. Her in my space, with her sweet honey scent. Her hand touching my thigh. The constant chatter all around us. My senses were now on overdrive. But instead of saying anything, I shook my head.

She raised a brow like she didn't believe me. Time to deflect.

"That's awesome that you've been invited to speak at that scholarship dinner."

She smiled up at me. "You heard that?"

I fought the urge to narrow my eyes at her. Of course I heard her. She was sitting right next to me, and it wasn't like she and Hattie were super quiet.

I nodded. "It's for women in science?"

"Yeah. It's a fundraising dinner. They've asked a few successful alumni to come back and speak."

"That's exciting."

She studied me almost like she wanted to say something. Why was she so surprised I listened to her? Said more about her ex than it did about me. Given the way I witnessed him speak to her, it wasn't shocking she expected her date to ignore her.

"So, Seth..." Savannah's voice reluctantly pulled my attention from Violet to where Savannah sat a few spots down. "Did you consider my T-shirt idea? I can totally design that. I bet it would raise a ton of money for the station." Her smirk had shit-stirrer written all over it.

This time there was no controlling my expression. I narrowed my eyes at her until she shrugged.

"You know what they say," she continued, "when life gives you lemons, grab some tequila and salt."

Violet chuckled as the blonde straight across from me said, "No one says that."

"I saw it on a sign." Savannah rolled her eyes. "So, someone has said it."

Violet chuckled again and I glanced that way, catching Hattie's look of bewilderment.

"Sometimes I wonder why she's friends with me and not her," Hattie said with a shake of her head.

"Aww, I find you funny too." Violet leaned toward her, bumping her shoulder. "Most of the time anyway."

I was a little confused. Why were we here celebrating Savannah's birthday if they weren't friends?

Multiple conversations started up again, and I was working to tune it all out, but a strange sound had me glancing back at Violet.

Did she just giggle?

She caught my gaze and angled over again even closer than last time. "I probably should've eaten something before that shot and margarita." She leaned further into me, resting her head on my shoulder.

I stiffened, but then immediately forced myself to relax. No one was going to believe we were dating if I tensed up every time she touched me. I shifted and placed my arm around her back, gripping her chair and pulling it closer. I wasn't quite sure what to do with my hand now though. The most convenient place would be on her hip, but that felt too intimate. So, I let it rest on the edge of her seat.

Thankfully, it wasn't long before the waitress and staff showed up with trays of food and passed the plates out. Because sitting there, ultra-aware of Violet nestled into my side, reminded me of the other two times she was pressed to my body.

And just like those other times, I couldn't say I hated it.

VIOLET

"Feeling better?" Seth's warm breath skated across my ear as his hand rubbed up and down my back, sending a shiver racing down my spine. It was hard to remember that this was fake when my body kept reacting to him in very real ways. Had I ever had such a quick and intense reaction like this to a man before?

I nodded, not trusting my voice to answer his question. Maybe I should have skipped the shot. At least I wasn't feeling so dizzy anymore. But I was definitely feeling all kinds of other things. Had the alcohol enhanced my body's reaction to him? Or was it just him?

And why did he have to smell so damn good? So rustic and manly. Rugged. Very Seth.

The food definitely helped me get my senses under control. I'd always been a lightweight when it came to alcohol, but on an empty stomach, it was ten times worse. I spun the green aventurine bracelet on my wrist, its properties of calm and balance probably helped decrease the effects of the alcohol as well. Hey, every little bit helps, right?

The waitress appeared again and handed Seth a glass of water.

"Thank you," he said before setting it down in front of me and moving my empty water out of the way. I hadn't even realized it was empty. "Try to drink more. It'll help."

I nodded and picked it up, bringing it to my lips.

"How long have you two been dating?" Hattie and Savannah's sister Ashley asked from across the table.

Shit. Didn't expect Ashley to be the one going straight for the jugular. At least the surprise didn't have me choking on my water. Seth and I hadn't talked about any of this. But it was always best to go with as close to the truth as possible.

I opened my mouth to respond, but Seth beat me to it. "A couple of weeks."

That was perfect, and exactly what I was going to say. I hid my smile behind my glass as I took another drink.

Ashley grinned, and I thought I caught a bit of a suggestive glint in her expression. "It was so obvious in that video as you carried her down the ladder. The way you held her close to you."

This time I actually coughed on the sip of water I'd just taken.

"But I am curious," she continued. "Why didn't you just climb down the ladder?"

Seth glanced over at me with a raised brow and a smirk pulling at his lips. It was a question that came up repeatedly in the comments on the video. And one I had no problem answering when people asked me in person. But no way was I about to engage with the trolls online who were looking for an easy rage-bait discussion about how I was too stupid to live.

"I'm afraid of heights, and I don't think he wanted to risk me panicking halfway down."

Seth cocked an eyebrow at me. "I wasn't sure you were climbing out that window without a plan."

That was probably true, although if it came down to it, I wouldn't have had a choice.

Hattie leaned over close to me. "Don't look, but James just walked in with Evelyn."

I stiffened, resisting the urge to turn around and glare at them.

Seth raised a brow but didn't miss a beat. His arm wound around my back and he pulled me tight to his side. His lips brushed my temple. "Do you want to go?"

I was grateful Savannah had invited me to come tonight, but I wasn't sure I wanted to stay now that James and the girl he'd cheated on me with were here. On the other hand, the whole point of fake dating Seth was to show James I'd moved on.

I looked up at Seth, unsure what I wanted to do.

He searched my face and gave me a clipped nod. "We'll stay a bit longer and then go. Okay?"

My body relaxed. "Yeah."

Seth made no attempt to move his arm. Instead, he brushed his hand up and down my bicep. I focused on the movement of his hand and the conversations around me, trying to ignore the fact that my cheating ex was there. I closed my eyes, letting Seth's touch ground me, and then laid my head against his shoulder.

I was just a little bit curious how Seth was still single. The guy brought me a freaking plant, made me a playlist, and was pretty amazing tonight. How attentive he was made it glaringly obvious how horrible James had been at that. And while I understood Seth didn't mean it the way a boyfriend would, it still made me wonder what his story was.

He definitely didn't like the attention from the women around town, which made me believe he wasn't looking for anything.

But when his gaze met mine, the intensity in his eyes made me wonder if he felt the little zaps of attraction between us too, or if he was just that good of an actor. My stomach flipped.

Dammit. Regardless of his story, I had to remember this was fake. Neither of us were looking for anything, and we'd agreed that this was a mutually beneficial plan.

I refused to mess it all up by reading into things that weren't there.

Chapter Fourteen

SETH

I PULLED up my text thread with Violet and my fingers hovered over the keys. We hadn't talked since I dropped her back off at her place Saturday night. Were there times that I found myself wanting to text her over the last few days? Yep. But each time I'd remind myself we weren't really dating.

Why that concept was getting harder and harder to remember, I didn't know. Okay, that wasn't the whole truth—I did know. I liked spending time with her. Maybe neither of us were ready for something serious again, but that didn't mean we couldn't be friends while we fake dated. Right?

Although the way I felt with her on Saturday, especially when she tensed up when James walked in, was anything but just friends. I hated that she couldn't seem to avoid him, but I was quickly learning that was part of small-town life. I could only hope that he was getting the message that she was mine now.

Fuck. I blinked. Not actually mine. But as far as he knew—as far as everyone knew—she was.

We'd made plans to get together for breakfast or lunch later in the week, but now I was curious what the latest development I'd overheard meant for the arson case. How fast news traveled in a small town still surprised me some days. I glanced at the time and typed out a quick message.

> Me: Heard the news. What does that mean for the arson case?

> Violet: Means we're pretty much starting over. Since we know the BBQ place wasn't the work of our arsonist, the matchbook Logan found isn't really a clue.

According to what Jay's wife said she'd heard, teenagers were responsible for that fire. When brought in with their parents to be questioned, they'd broken down and admitted it. They'd been using the abandoned place to lay low. Apparently, they didn't intentionally start the fire, but booze, cigarettes, and matches ended up being a bad combination.

> Me: I'm sorry.

> Violet: It's fine. Comes with the job. I'll eat a pint of ice cream and then I'll be ready to start over tomorrow.

I glanced over toward the kitchen where one of our paramedics, Kyle Williams, was pouring himself a cup of coffee. I'd recently made the connection that he was one of Hattie and Savannah's brothers. I got up and headed in his direction, leaning back on the counter next to him. He looked over at me with a raised brow.

"What was that ice cream place called?" I remembered him talking about it being the best in town when he and his wife were planning to take their kids after shift a few weeks ago.

"The Shack?"

"Right." I pushed away from the counter. "Thanks."

I ignored his grumbling as I walked away and sat back down in the chair I'd vacated a minute earlier, sending Violet another text.

> Me: Want to go to The Shack?

> Violet: Like together?

> Me: ...

> Violet: I thought you don't eat sugar?

> Me: Ice cream is the exception.

Mostly because I could never say no to my niece every time she asked me to have some with her. But I really hadn't had any since moving here. After the intense heat of the day, the frozen treat definitely sounded appealing.

> Violet: They have the best ice cream.

> Me: Is that a yes?

> Violet: Sure. Hopefully this kidnapping debacle doesn't take all night.

> Me: What?

What the hell? I was struggling to believe this small town could have a kidnapping. Then again, Hattie was abducted outside of her family's restaurant earlier this year by a crazed stalker, so anything was possible. But how come we hadn't heard of it yet?

I cursed under my breath when the alarms went off and

dispatch relayed the request for mutual aid for a wildfire in a neighboring town. We'd been dealing with our fair share in the last few weeks, I wasn't surprised others were too.

Depending on how bad this was, it could keep us past the end of shift.

Which meant ice cream might be out of the question for the evening. That had me grumbling the whole way downstairs because, dammit, I was really looking forward to seeing her again.

Chapter Fifteen

VIOLET

I STARED at the Ring camera footage hoping to get a glimpse of the offender. I'd wanted to smack Mrs. Jones when she came into the station earlier and announced, quite matter-of-factly, that she needed to file a kidnapping report.

The way the station went dead silent and stared at her was priceless.

I knew from the moment she stepped in the door she was about to send us on one of her godforsaken crusades. If it wasn't the feud with her neighbor about feeding the squirrels, it was people parking on the street in front of her house, or a million other different things she'd complain about.

Although this time an actual crime was committed—not kidnapping though, only theft.

But still, someone did in fact steal her precious garden gnomes. Hopefully she wasn't losing her mind and had just forgotten where she'd put them.

It took me long enough to get into her Ring account to even retrieve the footage. Of course she couldn't remember her password. Why did she even have the damn thing?

"Got you," I whispered to my computer screen.

An older man bent and picked up one of the gnomes before disappearing off camera. I downloaded that clip plus the three after it that showed the guy kidnapping all three of Mrs. Jones's yard décor family. I typed out a quick email to Dylan, attached the files, and hit send. My work here was done. He would be better at identifying the old guy since he pretty much knew everyone in town.

It was almost seven by then, and I assumed Seth would be getting off soon. I picked up my phone and shot off a text.

> Me: I'm about to leave work. Did you still want to get ice cream?

I waited a few minutes and then tucked my phone into my bag before heading out. I still hadn't heard anything by the time I got home, and since I hadn't eaten dinner yet, I busied myself in the kitchen warming up leftovers from the night before. My phone vibrated on the counter as I put the dishes in the dishwasher, and I grabbed a dishtowel to dry my hands before picking it up.

> Mountain Man: Can't make it tonight. Working a large wildfire. Gonna be a while.

> Me: Another one? We really need some rain.

> Mountain Man: Do you have a crystal for that? I'd totally carry that shit in my pocket if so.

I smiled as I stared at the screen. I hadn't told him anything about my healing crystals—not that they were any good for summoning rain—so I couldn't help but wonder how he knew about them.

> Me: Not specifically for rain, but citrine and green jade can attract good luck and success.

As I waited for Seth's reply, a text notification popped up from Hattie and I clicked on it.

> Hattie: Ok, so for Saturday it'll be you, me, my mom, and Savannah in one car. And then Ashley, Bella, Tina, and the girls in another. Rachel and Brittney are meeting us there since they live in the city already.

> Me: I'm so excited. I've never been wedding dress shopping before.

> Hattie: Really?

> Me: Yeah. I don't have sisters and I've only had one friend from college get married. She only took her mom and MOH dress shopping.

> Hattie: I'm glad you said yes, then.

> Me: Me too 😊

> Hattie: You and Seth looked pretty cozy on Saturday...you sure you two are just faking?

> Me: Yes. I'm sure. Neither of us are looking for anything serious. That's why we came up with this plan.

> Hattie: You could have something not serious.

> Me: I don't believe anything casual ever ends well. Someone always gets attached, feelings get hurt.

And I knew myself well enough to say it would be me. I would probably be the one to get attached. So a strict no-go boundary needed to be in place.

Hattie: You're probably right.

Hattie: Have you asked him about going to the scholarship fundraising dinner as your date?

Me: Not yet. I'm worried it's a little too serious to bring a fake date to.

Hattie: Maybe by then you'll be ready to bring a real date. 😉

I rolled my eyes. Talk about relentless. But the dinner wasn't for another five weeks, so I had plenty of time to decide if I wanted to ask him to be my fake date or not.

Chapter Sixteen

SETH

IT SUCKED that I hadn't been able to take Violet for ice cream. The fire had us all on site until well past ten. Maybe we could try again tonight. I made a mental note to text her once I was back at the station.

I opened the door to the small coffee shop and stepped inside. Unfortunately, I'd drawn the short straw for our coffee and pastry run. Out of all the things I hated when doing my job, this was one of them. I never could get in and out without someone attempting to talk to me.

Laughter drew my attention to a table in the corner. A group of women stared at me. One of them waved and... and did she just wink? Was she the same one who tried to give me her panties? I cringed at the memory.

A hand landed on my shoulder a second before Violet appeared next to me.

"Hey, babe." She popped up on her tiptoes and pressed her lips to my cheek.

Instinctively, I wound my arm around her back and pulled her closer into my side. "Hi." My voice sounded husky to my own ears, and I cleared it before glancing over her shoulder at the table full of women. Thankfully, they were no longer staring.

I breathed deeply, inhaling Violet's sweet scent, and stood frozen as she smiled up at me. Her dark purple lipstick held me captive.

"Are they still staring?" she whispered.

I blinked and loosened my hold on her waist. "No."

With a step back, she ran her hand down my arm, entwining our fingers, and moved forward to the counter, pulling me with her.

She immediately launched into small talk with the barista behind the counter, and after a moment, she waved her hand in my direction. "Go ahead and take his order first. He needs to get back to the station."

After I gave the girl my order, I looked over at Violet. "What did you want?"

She shook her head. "I'm doing a big order too."

The barista continued chatting with Violet as I paid for my order. We moved away from the counter after Violet ordered and paid for hers.

"Guess we both got stuck doing this," I voiced my thought out loud.

Her brow creased. "What do you mean?"

"The coffee run?"

"I volunteered."

I stared at her, completely bewildered. Who on earth would volunteer to do this? "Why? It's torture."

"You're adorable." She chuckled.

I rolled my eyes and folded my arms across my chest. We

had very different definitions of fun if she was intentionally heading into this caffeinated chaos. Didn't mean I wasn't interested in finding out what else she considered worthy of her time.

As we waited for our names to be called, I tried not to let my gaze wander down to the cleavage of her top. And failed. *Dammit.* What was wrong with me? She would end this whole fake dating thing if she caught me checking her out.

"You okay?"

I nodded. "Yeah." Maybe if I got her talking again I could focus on what she was saying and not anything else. Like how she smelled or her gorgeous round tits. *Fuck.* I shifted uncomfortably. "How's work going?"

She tilted her head and assessed me for a second before lifting her shoulders in a slight shrug. "It's fine. We have a meeting later with the lead arson investigator assigned to our case."

"Is that good or bad?"

"Just annoying. He's not going to tell us anything we don't already know. The state doesn't have the manpower right now to dedicate someone to help us. And until we have something else to bring him here, there's nothing any of us can do anyway. We need a solid piece of evidence to get them to commit their resources to our case."

I thought about what she said and then shook my head. "I don't get it. Logan finding the matchbook and the arsonist setting his garage on fire seems like more than a coincidence. Isn't it still relevant evidence based on that?"

"Yes and no. I'm personally not ruling the Taylors out. We just can't justify it as a piece of evidence because it wasn't found at one of the fires actually set by the arsonist. Suspicious coincidence? Yes. But even still, the matchbook wouldn't be evidence we could use. We need something else. Or something pointing us to another suspect."

I nodded. That made sense.

My name was called, and I moved to the counter to grab the

order. I hung back next to Violet as she waited for her order, and once she had hers in hand, we headed out onto the sidewalk.

"How about ice cream tonight?" I asked as we stood outside of the large window of the coffee shop.

"Sure. Text me when you're off shift."

I nodded and glanced through the window, catching the women staring again. I started to lean forward, intent on kissing her on the cheek, but before I could, she popped up on her tiptoes and pressed her lips quickly against mine.

It was a chaste brush of her lips, but it awakened every nerve ending in my body.

She smiled. "See you later, Mountain Man."

I stood stock still as she turned and walked away. The need to really kiss her penetrated deep, and I cursed under my breath.

She wasn't ready to date, I reminded myself, and to be honest, I wasn't sure I was either. If I said it enough, eventually it would sink in.

Chapter Seventeen

VIOLET

As I expected, the arson investigator had nothing useful to tell us other than to start back at the beginning. So Dylan and Aiden had started canvassing again and I'd watched hours upon hours of video footage. This would be my life for the foreseeable future, or until we found something.

Thankfully, I could leave for the night and go get ice cream with Seth. I smiled thinking about earlier at the coffee shop. The surprise on his face when I'd given him a quick kiss. I'd seen him noticing the women looking at us, and I'd just assumed he was leaning in to kiss me. But then he'd stared back at me in surprise… and something else I couldn't discern.

Oh well. Hopefully, I hadn't made things awkward.

I continued through the police station and out the door that led to the sidewalk. I glanced both ways before spotting Seth leaning against the front of his car a few spots away. He looked up and sent me a smirk. One I wasn't sure I'd seen yet.

Actually, that was a lie. It was similar to the one he'd given me at dinner Saturday night when Ashley asked me why I hadn't just climbed down the ladder.

"You ready?"

I nodded. "I'm always ready for ice cream."

He grunted and opened the passenger door. Nothing felt awkward, thankfully. And the playlist he'd made me was already playing from his car's speakers. I smiled thinking about him listening to it even when I wasn't in the car with him.

He pulled out into traffic and glanced over at me. "Do you get the same thing or change it up?"

"I am definitely a mood ice cream eater." That new coffee drink I'd ordered earlier made me want something with caramel. "I'll probably get their salted caramel."

He chuckled. "That doesn't surprise me since you ordered that brown sugar caramel latte today. Are you a pumpkin spice girl too?"

Wow. He literally didn't miss anything. Was he that observant with everyone else or just me? "Will you think less of me if I said yes?"

"Not at all." He lifted his hand from the steering wheel and pinched his thumb and forefinger together, almost but not quite touching. "Well, maybe a little tiny bit."

I rolled my eyes. Silence followed, and I was surprised I didn't feel the need to fill it with useless chatter. Maybe because I was starting to understand he liked lulls in conversation. That just sitting and listening to music, or being in a big group, observing and listening, felt more like his speed, so I didn't need to constantly find things to talk about.

It was...refreshing. Almost relaxing.

I sat back and closed my eyes listening to "Feel Like This" by

Abra. Some of the songs he picked I wouldn't have thought I'd like, but I actually did.

I still hadn't gotten over that he made me a playlist. I glanced over at him, studying him, and wondering again what his story was.

"How come you're still single?" tumbled from my lips without much thought.

His back went ramrod straight. *Shit.* Whatever it was, it didn't seem like something he wanted to talk about.

But then he sighed, and his shoulders relaxed just a bit. "I had a girlfriend in Charlotte."

Was that part of the reason he moved here? "What happened?"

His hands gripped the steering wheel tighter, making his knuckles turn white. "I thought I'd give her a ring and we'd move here together. She wasn't thinking the same thing."

"Oh." I could definitely relate to that feeling of a rug being pulled out from under you. "I'm sorry."

He shrugged. "It happens. I probably should be happy I found out when I did that she wasn't as invested as I was."

"At least your ex isn't here harassing you to get back together."

He glared over at me. "Is he still bothering you?"

I chuckled at the overprotectiveness in his voice. "No, not anymore. I think he finally got the message." But I still couldn't seem to avoid him.

"Good." He nodded.

We were quiet again as the minutes passed, and it wasn't long until he was pulling into The Shack's lot. After he parked, we got out and fell in step next to each other as we made our way to the small building to order. I expected him to order vanilla or chocolate, maybe Rocky Road, and I couldn't stop the laugh that bubbled up and slipped past my lips when he requested birthday cake.

He shrugged. "It's my niece's favorite. I was only allowed to order that anytime we went for ice cream."

I shook my head. Being bossed around by a tiny human definitely did not fit the whole mountain man persona. Maybe I needed to consider changing his nickname.

"She's scary when she doesn't get her way," he added.

"If you say so."

Ice creams in hand, we sat down at one of the picnic tables scattered around the grassy area of the lot.

"Want to try mine?" I reached my cone out toward him.

His nose scrunched like he smelled something bad.

"Never mind, Mr. Serious." I chuckled.

Before I could pull my arm back, he grabbed my hand, bringing the ice cream to his mouth, and took a bite. "Not bad. And what happened to Mountain Man?"

I shrugged. "Nothing. Just depends on what mood I'm in whether you're Mr. Serious or Mountain Man."

He extended his arm across the table. "Your turn to try mine."

I leaned forward and took a slow lick of his ice cream. His gaze zeroed in on my mouth and suddenly the air grew tense as his gaze darkened.

The ringing of his phone broke through the moment, and he looked down at it.

"Sorry, mind if I take this? It's my niece." When his gaze met mine, there wasn't any of the desire I thought I saw a moment earlier.

Was I just reading into it?

"No, not at all. Go ahead." I nodded to the phone on the table that displayed a little red-headed girl in pigtails.

He picked it up and a huge smile lit his face as he answered the video call. I wasn't sure I'd seen him that animated before.

"Are you eating ice cream?" The little voice said.

He nodded. "Yes. Your favorite."

"Dad said you're coming home this weekend for Poppop's and Granny's anniversary party?"

"Yes, I'll be there. Told you last time we talked that I would."

"Can you take me to get ice cream?"

His smile fell just slightly. "We can try. No promises though. With the party happening, we're going to have a busy day."

"Okaaay..." she said with a slight whine to her voice. "Why are you at a playground?"

Seth looked over his shoulder toward the climbing structure and swings then glanced back at the phone. "It's for the ice cream place that I'm at." He turned his phone, slowly scanning the area. "See...they have tables and stuff."

"Who's that?"

He smiled over at me before holding the phone so she could see both of us. "This is Violet."

"Is she your girlfriend?"

He chuckled. "Yeah, kinda."

I didn't know what to think of his admission. Technically, he didn't need to tell his niece—or family for that matter—the lie. But maybe that was easier than explaining the truth.

"Dani, time for bed," a woman called, followed by the little girl whining that she wasn't tired.

"Better go get ready for bed." Seth's serious face was back. "You don't want to get in trouble."

"But I'm not tired."

He raised his brows at her and she huffed. "Fine."

I fought the chuckle that wanted to slip past my lips. It was times like these that made me envious of other people having siblings. I would be a kick-ass fun Aunt Violet.

SETH

"I guess tonight was kinda pointless," Violet said as we made our way back to the car.

Pointless? What did she mean? I froze midstep, and when she looked back at me, I searched her face for the answer.

"You know, because no one was here to see us."

Right. The whole fake dating thing. I was doing a crap job remembering that was what we were doing. I hadn't thought about that at all tonight. I enjoyed just spending time with her.

"Maybe we can grab lunch on Friday."

"That'd be good."

I opened her car door, and my hand tightened on the frame as she brushed past me to climb in. Shutting the door as she turned away from me to buckle in, I took a deep breath before heading around to my side.

"Will you be here Sunday for the annual softball game?"

I nodded. "I'll be on duty, not playing."

"You did that on purpose, I'm assuming?"

"Chief wanted a mix of full-time guys and volunteers on the team, and then a mix on shift. Jay, Adam, and Zack really wanted to play, so Logan and I offered to be on shift."

She tilted her head and studied me. I wasn't sure why she was looking at me like I'd surprised her. I didn't care if I played or not, so it made more sense to offer to work so the guys who wanted to play could.

"We weren't given that option. There's only like fourteen or so of us, barely enough to make a team. And no volunteers to call in."

"They have to have someone on shift."

She nodded. "Yeah, Ethan and Tim are on patrol. The rest of us are playing. Well, besides Martha. She said she's too old. Although she's not even sixty yet."

I pulled into the small parking lot next to the police station where Violet's car was parked.

"Thanks again for the ice cream."

I gave her a clipped nod. "I'll text you about lunch on Friday."

"Sounds good." She hesitated for a moment, running her tongue along her bottom lip.

And I couldn't stop myself from tracking the movement. My gaze drifted slowly up to meet hers, but only for a heartbeat before she pulled it away and reached for the handle of the door.

She shut the door, and I groaned as I watched her walk to her car. The realization that I was screwed hit me like a punch to the gut. Because, dammit, I was actually starting to like this chick.

I scrubbed a hand down my face. Did I even want to go down that road again? Shaking my head, I reminded myself that even if I did, there wasn't anything I could do about it.

Yet.

Chapter Eighteen

SETH

I RELAXED BACK in the chair, bringing the beer to my mouth and smiling at the scene in front of me before taking a sip. My brother's dog stood above Dani, licking her face as she giggled.

The screen door opened, and Mason stepped out. He took the seat next to me, his own beer in hand. We sat there quietly, watching Dani run around in the backyard. The party for my parents was over and everyone had left to head home except for me. But since I was on shift tomorrow, I needed to head back soon.

"Mom asked me if you're dating someone. I had no fucking clue what to say. 'He's fake dating some chick to avoid all the single women in town' didn't seem right."

I rolled my eyes. "A simple no would have been fine."

Although Violet and I had gone on another lunch *date* the day before, we weren't actually dating.

"Seriously? You know how she is. Especially because she thinks you are."

I cocked a brow his way. "Why would she think that?"

My brother shrugged. "Probably because you kept smiling at your phone. Only thing that usually makes you smile is Dani. Well, at least since things ended with Lucy."

I scoffed. He was almost as dramatic as his daughter. It wasn't like I could just ignore Violet's texts. And I found her story telling about Mrs. Jones and the older man who lived next to her entertaining. But I couldn't deny that she made me smile.

I caught his expectant look. Did he want a response to that? "It's complicated."

"No shit?" He smirked. "Did you not think that could be a possibility? You were so certain spending time with a woman you find attractive wouldn't eventually lead to wanting more than a fake dating relationship?"

"At the time, no, that didn't cross my mind."

"And now?"

I lifted my beer to my mouth and thought through his question as I took another drink. "It doesn't matter what I want. She's still getting over her ex and isn't looking to date someone right now."

"But if she did want more?"

I sighed and lifted my shoulders in a slight shrug. "She's easy to be around."

I didn't know any other way to explain it. Even though she would give me shit from time to time, I didn't feel like I had to constantly fill the space between us with endless chatter. I liked that. But I still wasn't sure I wanted something serious again. At least not anytime soon.

He studied me, giving me that brotherly look that said I was about to get some unsolicited advice. "I think Mom might be onto something. You like this girl." He shot me a smirk before relaxing back in his chair.

He was quiet, and I kept waiting for him to say more. Typically, I'd be fine with the silence, but this was killing me. Maybe because I wanted his opinion.

"What? No advice, big brother?"

He chuckled. "I don't think you need advice. You're smart and you care. More than most people realize." He tipped his bottle in my direction. "I think you already know what you should do and you're just waiting for the right time."

I sat there digesting that until Shelby came out the door and headed into the yard. She didn't glance our way, and when I looked over at Mason, he looked at her with sadness in his eyes.

"Things still rough?" I asked in a low voice.

He nodded. "At this point I feel like I'm just walking on eggshells. She's unhappy, and I don't think I can fix it."

"What does she say?"

"That I'm not listening to her. But I'm trying."

Listening had never been Mason's best quality. He was the talker, the doer, while I sat back and watched and listened. Probably why I got better grades and he excelled more at sports.

I wasn't sure I could offer much advice. "Have you talked about therapy?"

He huffed. "I suggested that once and she accused me of being resentful of her going back to work full time."

"Are you?"

He shot me a look of disbelief. "Seriously?"

I shrugged. "Just asking."

"No. Not at all. But I think *she's* unhappy about working full time again and just can't or won't admit it. And I just don't know what else to say or do to make it better. I feel like everything I do is the wrong thing."

"I'm sorry, man." I didn't really know what else to say, so we both remained quiet until Shelby and Dani approached.

111

"Uncle Seth," the little ball of energy called. "Did you see my cartwheel?"

"I did. You're getting so good at those."

"I've been practicing."

"I bet." I stood and stretched. "I better get going."

"Aww, man. Do you have to?" she pouted.

"Yeah. I have to work early tomorrow."

"Fine." She crossed her arms with a huff.

I knelt down to her level. "Hey, how about I come visit one day later in the week and we go get ice cream?" Since she was with my parents while Mason and Shelby were at work, and she didn't start school for another week, I could easily come visit on Wednesday or Thursday when I was off.

"Promise?"

"I promise I'll try."

"Okay." She gave me a hug and then ran inside.

I said my goodbyes to Mason and Shelby and started my drive home. A smile pulled at my lips as I thought about tomorrow and the softball game. I'd be lying if I said I wasn't looking forward to seeing Violet.

Chapter Nineteen

SETH

"WANT to swing by the softball game?" I glanced over at Logan as he pulled the rig away from the possible gas leak call we'd just finished with.

He looked over at me with a raised brow. "Seriously?"

"Why not?" I'd figured he'd want to stop by at some point and cheer on the team. But maybe not. He was more like me than the other guys. Neither of us preferred large social situations over small groups of people. But I didn't make a habit of breaking promises if I could avoid it. "I told Violet we'd try to stop by."

He chuckled. "Right. Violet."

The way he said her name was laced with suspicion. He could think what he wanted, but it didn't change the fact that I didn't want to disappoint her.

He studied me for a minute and then shrugged. "Yeah, we can swing by."

I tried not to smile, but I was struggling to tamp down my excitement at the idea of getting to see her. As Logan pulled the rig along the curb at the back of the parking lot, I searched the field hoping for a glance of Violet. I reached for the handle and froze, looking over at Logan who sat eyeing me with a knowing smirk.

He shook his head and chuckled. "Come on, boys. Let's go so Romeo here can see his girl."

I'd never been this excited to watch any kind of athletic game. Sports wasn't my go-to entertainment choice. And honestly, I had no interest in the game itself. Only in seeing Violet. Images of her in a button-up jersey—her breasts pushing against the buttons, threatening to pop them open—crossed my mind. I shifted on my feet, willing my dick to not misbehave.

The three volunteers we were paired with took spots on the bleachers, while Logan and I stood near the fence surrounding the softball field. The Donut Dodgers were up to bat. If I thought their name was stupid, ours was worse—the Red Hot Responders. Like who the fuck came up with these names?

Violet was standing on first base, and if I knew her at all at this point, I'd bet she thought the names were cute. I made a mental note to not call them fucking stupid to her face. As I expected, the whole team wore matching jerseys, each personalized with their last names. Pearson was printed across the back of Violet's. The fire department had on similar jerseys too.

She looked my way with a smile and a wave, and I gave her a quick tip of my head. She leaned over, bracing her hands on one knee, ready to run to second when it was time. I zeroed in on one of our young volunteers, who was the current first baseman, staring at Violet's ass.

The insanely tight leggings she wore were like a second skin, but that didn't mean this tool needed to be staring. Did he not know she had a boyfriend?

Fake boyfriend.

But no one else but us knew that.

"Who's the assclown on first?" I asked Logan.

"Daniel?" He glanced over at me and cocked a brow. "Why do you look like you're about to murder someone?" He followed my gaze. "Ahh. I see."

I couldn't hear what, but Daniel must have said something because Violet sent him a smirk.

Damn. Was she flirting back?

"Dude." Logan nudged me. "Relax. He's harmless."

Harmless my ass.

Violet caught my eye and tilted her head, assessing me. A heartbeat later, Daniel looked over too. I took the opportunity to narrow my eyes and rest my hands on my hips, silently telling him to back the fuck off. His eyes widened and he took a couple of steps back.

Good. Message received.

"I guess I was wrong about you two." Logan chuckled.

"What?"

"Based on the death glares you're sending that poor kid, you're obviously really into her. He's probably pissing his pants right now."

"Good. He should learn to keep his eyes off other people's girls."

Dylan stepped up to bat and hit the ball way out to left field. Violet sprinted quickly around the bases, getting PD a run.

My feet were moving before I even realized what I was doing. I stepped up close to the bench just as Violet made her way toward the end.

"I thought you were on shift," she said, still studying me.

"I am. We just finished a call and thought we'd swing by to watch some of the game."

She raised a brow. "You don't look very happy about it."

Logan chuckled behind me, and I sent him a glare over my shoulder.

I looked down, kicking at the grass with the toe of my boot. How could I possibly explain that I was jealous? Jesus. I didn't even understand it. She wasn't even mine. She'd think I was insane.

A sound, almost like a snicker, hit my ears and I whipped my gaze up to see Aiden standing behind Violet. "He's not happy about that young buck out there eyeing up his girl." He walked further down the bench, laughing darkly.

"His girl?" Violet's eyes widened and her lips parted as she stared back at me. "Oh." Her demeanor changed, switching to the actress role I'd come to recognize when others were around, and she waved off the comment. "Don't worry babe, I only have eyes for you." She stepped closer, placing her palms against my chest and popping up on her tiptoes.

Not this time. She was going to fake kiss me, keep it all within the act we needed to keep up, but I wanted to find out how soft her lips were for real.

I reached up and cupped the back of her head, holding her a few inches from my face. "Everyone's watching," I whispered, not knowing if anyone was actually watching or not. Either way, I didn't care. "Better make it good."

Her brows rose high on her forehead. "Yeah," she breathed out.

I brought her closer, tilting my head, and slowly brushed my lips against hers. Once, twice, a third time—just because I wasn't ready for it to end yet. She sighed against my mouth as I broke the kiss and pulled back.

Now that I'd gotten a taste, a real taste, I wanted more.

I shouldn't. I couldn't. But I did.

Chapter Twenty

VIOLET

"Like, he *kissed* me, kissed me."

I finished laying out the amethyst points on my coffee table and looked across at Hattie. I really didn't think she understood what I was trying to say. Not that I even understood how I felt. Other than when he'd kissed me it made my body tingle in all the right places, and then I had to act like it didn't just make my legs feel shaky. Luckily, I didn't have to endure standing there and overanalyzing the way he looked at me afterwards—like he wanted to do it again—because we got another out and I had to head to the outfield.

"Oh, I know. I'm pretty sure the whole town saw that kiss." She picked up each crystal, turning them over in her hand. "These are gorgeous."

"You like 'em?" I'd asked her if I could make amethyst necklaces for all the bridesmaids, to go with the purple dresses she'd picked out the prior weekend. She loved the idea, and I was thankful I had something else to focus on besides my asshole ex, my fake relationship that was starting to feel not so fake, and the arson investigation that had stalled again.

"Yes. They're perfect." She picked up her wineglass and brought the rose-colored liquid to her mouth, taking a sip. "So what's your problem with the kiss?"

I shook my head, not sure how to explain it. "It, umm, didn't feel fake, and I can't stop thinking about it."

She chuckled. "And how is that a problem?"

I rolled my eyes. "Wanting to kiss my fake boyfriend for real kind of defeats the purpose of the whole plan, remember?"

"Or you change the plan. Give yourself the opportunity to explore whatever is between you two. Because based on what I saw, there's definitely something there."

It was more complicated than that. Neither of us were in the right place for a relationship, right?

"He's getting over an ex, too. And maybe the kiss didn't affect him the way it did me."

Hattie laughed. "Girl, Dylan said he thought Seth was going to stomp out onto that field, throw you over his shoulder, and go all caveman on poor Daniel."

At first, I didn't even understand why Seth was glaring. Once Aiden mentioned it, I just assumed he was playing his part. Then he kissed me and my mind turned to muck. And now? Now I wasn't sure of anything. Maybe he was just better at this pretending crap than I was.

"Look, stop stressing." Hattie reached over and covered my hands where I was focused on twisting the wire around one of the crystals. "Just let things unfold the way they're meant to."

"Now you sound like me."

"Good. Bring on the positivity and joy and good luck of all your stones and the universe."

I chuckled. "We're supposed to go out again Friday night."

"What crystal did you say is good for opening the heart to new love?"

I pointed to the delicate pink stone that sat in one of the trays. "Rose quartz."

"Wear that Friday night," she said with a wink.

I sighed and picked up the semi-precious gem. Could I be open to the idea of dating? Of a new relationship? New love?

I didn't believe Seth would ever intentionally hurt me, but I wasn't sure I was ready to put my heart on the line again.

The thing that scared me the most was I could easily see myself falling for a guy like Seth.

Chapter Twenty-One

SETH

WEDNESDAY 9:52 A.M.

> Me: Logan wants us to go out with him and Izzy Friday night.

> Violet: And what did you say?

> Me: No. But he won't leave it alone. Says you'd enjoy it.

> Violet: Lol. I mean that could be fun. But we don't have to.

Me: Just told him yes. They want to go to The Crescent Moon. Says they have live music on Fridays.

Violet: Wow. Pretty sure that's the most words I've seen you use.

Me: Ha. Ha.

Violet: So, live music? Does that mean dancing? Because I love dancing.

Me: I don't dance.

Violet: That doesn't surprise me.

Violet: You live a very boring life.

Me: I did. Until I had to carry your ass down a ladder.

Violet: And you're welcome. Now you're having more fun.

Me: Sigh.

Violet: Secretly you love it.

Me: I'll pick you up at 7 on Friday.

Violet: Ok Mountain Man.

Me: And we're back to that.

Violet: 😏

Chapter Twenty-Two

VIOLET

SETH HELD the door to The Crescent Moon open, and a shiver raced down my spine as he stared at me. My feet slowed. Actually, everything seemed to slow down.

Things felt different. I couldn't explain it, but there was this tension between us.

Was it new? Or had I just never noticed it before?

I stepped inside and he placed his hand on the small of my back as we weaved through the crowded bar, seeking out Logan and Izzy. I was suddenly ultra-aware of his touch. Like the way his gaze had lingered as it ran over me.

"There," he said, leaning down until his chin grazed my cheekbone. His warm breath against my ear had heat pooling low in my belly. "In the corner."

He led me to the right and I spotted the couple at a high top.

Logan smirked. "Wasn't sure if you guys were actually going to come."

Seth grumbled as he pulled out a chair and I climbed up on it.

"What do you want to drink?" he asked, so close a mix of leather and wood enveloped me.

"Cranberry and vodka."

He raised an eyebrow. "Probably should order an appetizer too." He lifted his hand, attempting to flag down a waitress.

Once we all ordered drinks and a plate of nachos, I fiddled with the light pink pendant hanging around my neck.

Izzy tipped her chin in my direction. "My friend Lyla has a few of your crystal pieces. That one you're wearing is pretty. What is it?"

"Rose quartz." I still couldn't believe I listened to Hattie and wore it tonight.

"Lyla said she just ordered a black tourmaline pendant because of its protective and resilient benefits." Izzy angled her head to the side. "What does rose quartz do?"

"Oh, umm…" I could feel Seth's eyes trained on me. "It can do a lot. Helps with emotional pain, eases stress, enhances confidence."

"You make those?" Logan asked.

"She has a shop on Etsy," Seth answered quickly.

I glanced over at him, again wondering how he knew that, and made a mental note to ask him. "I've been making them since I was a teenager. My mom was really into essential oils, healing crystals, and incense, so I learned from her and started designing jewelry with them."

The waitress appeared, setting the nachos and our drinks down.

"What would you suggest for me?" Izzy asked as the waitress walked away.

I studied her carefully, only knowing a little bit about her. But her wide smile and carefree attitude was enough for me to give her a suggestion. "I would suggest citrine. It's my personal favorite. It's literally called the happy stone because it promotes joy and positivity. You could pair it with an amethyst that will offer calm among chaos."

"That's the one she needs." Logan smirked as he brought a piece of nacho to his mouth.

She swatted at his chest. "Are you trying to say I'm chaotic?"

"You signed us up for ten dozen cookies for the bake sale tomorrow."

She rolled her eyes. "And the girls and I got them all done today, didn't we?"

"You sure did." He kissed her temple, and I couldn't help but smile. They were too cute.

"So are the girls back in school now?" I grabbed another nacho from the plate, popping it in my mouth.

"There's a back-to-school thing and bake sale tomorrow. School starts Monday." Izzy took a sip from her cider before placing it back down on the table.

Seth was quiet as usual as we chatted, only adding in here and there, but his presence next to me was unmoving. It was comforting to know he was attentive, even if not talkative.

As I finished the last of my drink, Izzy suddenly jumped up from the table. "Oh. I love this song." She grabbed my arm and pulled me off my stool. "Come on, let's dance."

Was Logan not much of a dancer either?

We left them behind to find a good spot on the crowded dance floor. The music was a good mix, and we were having a great time in our own little bubble, until two guys slowly made their way into our space.

They acted harmless enough, maybe a little drunk, but I didn't even have a chance to assess their intentions when Izzy's voice pulled my attention to her.

"And here comes caveman one and two."

I followed her gaze back toward our table. Seth and Logan

were headed straight toward us, death glares aimed at the guys near us. Izzy giggled as Logan pulled her into his arms.

I didn't really know what Seth would do. Excitement coursed through me as he took my hand and spun me, bringing me back against his chest.

"Thought you said you don't dance?" I shot him a smirk over my shoulder.

"I don't."

I chuckled at the contradiction because he was, in fact, dancing with me. He moved us slowly, swaying back and forth. I was overwhelmed by the sensations his touch was causing. The way his fingers dug into my hip and his body pressed tightly to my back.

I closed my eyes as his fingers brushed along my side. My core throbbed, wishing I could find out how his touch would feel on other parts of my body. His warm breath skated across my ear sending goose bumps down my arms.

"Want another drink?" he asked.

I nodded, hoping that would ease the need gathering in my belly. He stepped away and instantly I missed the connection. I tracked him as he flagged down the waitress and ordered us more drinks. I took a moment to look around, noticing the guys from earlier had their own dance partners.

Izzy yanked on my arm as the song changed again. "I love Sugarland."

Country wasn't one of my favorites, but I did like this particular song. Seth was back and smirking at me as Izzy and I danced and lip-synced the lyrics. I could relate to "Settlin'" at the moment. After the mess with James, I had no intention of settling for anything less than what I deserved.

Seth leaned forward, so close to my ear that his words made goose bumps break out on my arms again. "Thought you didn't like country?"

"I said some of it was okay."

"I definitely remember you saying it was mostly depressing."

"Mostly is the key word." I sent him a playful smile and squeaked when he pinched my side. I swatted at him, and he grabbed my hand, pulling me closer and swaying us again to the music. For someone who said he didn't dance, he was doing a damn good job at it.

The waitress placed our drinks down on our table a moment later and I nodded that way. "She brought our drinks."

"Are you done dancing?"

I pressed my teeth into my bottom lip. Did I want to stop dancing with him? That was a complicated question. I liked the idea that I could flirt with him and not have to worry about if he wanted it to go further. But also, I could use a break from the way he was causing my body to come alive in ways I wasn't even sure James ever had.

"For now."

He turned us, placing his hand on the small of my back, and led me back to the table.

I could feel his gaze on me as I sipped my drink, and I peeked up at him. If I weren't sitting on a stool, I probably would have stumbled back. The way he was looking at me was unlike anything I'd ever experienced.

Desire and need swam in his eyes, matching my own. One night together was a bad idea, but it didn't stop me from wondering what it would be like.

SETH

I tipped my beer bottle toward Violet's necklace. "Isn't rose quartz the love stone?"

Was it dumb that part of me hoped her wearing that particular gem meant she was opening herself up to the idea of a new relationship? Was that what I wanted? I sure as hell didn't like the idea of her starting anything with someone else. That became glaringly obvious after the softball game last week when I thought Daniel was flirting. And it hit me again earlier in the evening when I imagined her dancing with one of those guys who'd made their way over. In fact, the thought of her with another guy made me see red.

She nodded and tilted her head, studying me. "How do you know about the stones?"

"Lyla mentioned you make jewelry." I shrugged. "I was curious, so I looked it up."

She opened her mouth and then shut it again. My gaze drifted down to her lips, covered in a dark crimson red. I forced myself to look away. Tonight was utter hell. Touching her like I had when we danced, having her pressed against me—it was all perfection and misery at the same time.

A second later, Logan and Izzy took their seats. Well, Logan sat back on his stool. Izzy was almost in his lap rather than on her own stool.

He whispered something in her ear and an obvious blush rose to her cheeks.

"We're going to get the check and head home," Logan said as he raised his hand, signaling the waitress.

It was apparent the reason they were rushing home. I would be lying if I said I didn't want to do the same with Violet. I shifted uncomfortably, willing my dick to not make a scene as I tried to push away thoughts of plowing into her. How her plump lips would part as she moaned my name, her perfect tits bouncing each time I drove into her.

I blinked and bit back a groan. Jesus. I really needed to get my shit together. I'd never had such a visceral reaction to a woman before, and I had no idea how to handle it.

Once we paid the check and were alone at the table, Violet and I sat, continuing to nurse our drinks.

"Did you have a good time?" I asked.

Her gaze met mine, holding me captive as she searched my face. For what, I wasn't sure. Did she feel the same thing between us tonight that I did? Was she questioning it?

"Yeah." She ran her tongue along her bottom lip, and I tracked the movement, swallowing down a groan that bubbled up as I was inundated with memories of the kiss we'd shared last weekend at the softball game.

Noticing her drink was now empty, I downed the last of my beer. "You ready to go?"

She pulled her lower lip into her mouth with her teeth and sent me a slight nod. Neither of us said a word as we made our way to the car and I drove toward her townhome. Obviously, I knew what my issue was. I wanted an excuse to kiss her. In truth, I wanted so much more than that. But I had no intention of screwing up something real between us by having one night together.

Why was she so quiet, though? Was she having the same thoughts?

I parked in front of her townhome and looked over at her. All the air left my lungs at the desire that stared back at me. But it was mixed with so much hesitation and uncertainty, it just cemented the conclusion I'd already come to.

I couldn't let this happen. Not tonight. Not yet. And if she asked if I wanted to come in, I wasn't sure I was strong enough to say no.

"Thanks for coming out tonight." I choked out the words, hating what I had to do. "Do you want to grab coffee or lunch one day this week?"

Hopefully, that was enough to remind her of our plan, without sounding like a total dick. Her brows pulled together, and I saw the moment in her eyes when she put us firmly back into the fake dating category.

I wanted to scream *No, don't. Invite me in,* but I couldn't.

"Yeah, I'll text you." She grabbed the handle, not even glancing over at me as she opened the door and slipped out. "Goodnight, Seth."

"Goodnight."

I sat frozen, hands gripping the steering wheel until she was safely inside her house. Because every fiber in my being wanted to go after her.

Chapter Twenty-Three

SETH

IT HAD BEEN three days since I dropped Violet off at her house Friday night, and every day since then I wanted to call or text her. But the problem was I had no clue where to go from there. I put my other earbud in and pushed play before raising my ax and bringing it down in the center of a piece of wood, splintering it in half.

It wasn't like I needed the wood yet. It was still August, so I wasn't planning on using my fireplace. But the task helped keep my body busy while I struggled to calm my mind. I put another log in front of me and brought the ax down hard again.

After ten more pieces, I pulled my phone out, not able to stop thinking about her.

> Me: How's your day going?

After ten minutes with no reply, I typed out another message.

> Me: Want to grab lunch or coffee or something one day this week?

What felt like forever, but was probably only twenty minutes later, she responded.

> Violet: I'm home sick today. I'll let you know once I'm feeling better.

Home sick? Was that just an excuse? Had she decided she didn't want to do this anymore? The thought sat like lead in my gut.

I jumped in the shower and swung by the store on the way to her place. I needed to know. If I needed to, I would lay my cards on the table. Because the thought of not seeing her felt like someone just sucker punched me in the stomach.

I knocked on her door, and after a minute the door swung open. Violet stood, wrapped in a blanket, skin pale and free of any makeup.

Jesus. I thought she was beautiful with all that dark shit on her face, but this Violet was breathtaking. Except it was obvious she really wasn't feeling well.

"What are you doing here?"

"Wanted to check on you." I held up the grocery bag in my hand. "I got you stuff from the store."

I took a step forward and she sighed, opening the door wider and stepping out of the way. "Seth, I don't want to get you sick. I'm fine. It's just the flu or something."

I didn't give a shit if she got me sick. I reached out and placed the back of my hand on her forehead. Fuck. She was burning up.

"Have you taken anything?"

She shook her head. "Not since early this morning."

"Come on." I wrapped my arm around her shoulders and led her to her couch. "I wasn't sure what flavor Gatorade you liked, so I got four different ones."

She sent me a weak smile. "Red is fine."

I opened the cold medicine and handed her the two capsules before opening the red bottle of Gatorade and handing her that as well. "Have you eaten anything today?"

She shook her head.

"Think you can try some soup if I make it?"

"Seth, you don't have to do—"

"Violet, I'm not leaving."

She sighed. "Fine, it's your funeral. Don't say I didn't warn you."

"Well, if I get sick, then you can come take care of me."

She laid her head back against the top of the cushion and closed her eyes. "What soups do you have?"

"Chicken noodle, chicken and rice, or vegetable."

"Chicken noodle, please."

I wanted to sit with her and hold her, but she needed to eat too. She didn't open her eyes or look back at me, so I went into the kitchen and started heating up the soup.

I smiled as my gaze landed on the African Violet. It looked like it was thriving, and I loved that she was actually taking care of it. Lucy used to forget about them and would end up killing them.

After I finished heating up the soup, I brought it back into the living room. "Here you go."

Violet lifted her head and sat up straight, taking the bowl from my hands. "Thank you."

"You're welcome." I sat down next to her, looking her over. Her hair was pulled up into a messy bun, and the color was coming back to her face a little.

The blanket she'd wrapped around her shoulders had dropped to her waist when she sat up. I froze as my gaze ran over the front of her loose-fitting white T-shirt, curious if she was wearing a bra. The material pulled against her breast as she moved her hand to her mouth, taking a bite of soup. The outline of her nipple—along with something else—became visible before she moved her arm again and the shirt relaxed against her once more. I couldn't be sure, but was it a nipple piercing I thought I saw? My dick seemed to like that idea very much, and the urge to find out was overwhelming.

I shifted uncomfortably. The last thing she needed was me sporting a hard-on while she was sick.

Pull it together, Davis.

She stole a glance over at me. "You know you really don't have to do all this. It's not like you're my real boyfriend or anything." She chuckled awkwardly, leaning forward and placing her bowl on the table.

I locked my jaw tight. Because—fuck me—I wanted that damn title. But this wasn't the moment to make that declaration.

"I know, but I want to. Besides, I need you better by this weekend."

She tilted her head, and her brows pulled together. "Why? What's this weekend?"

"The Labor Day parade and block party thing?"

"Oh. Right." Her brows were still furrowed. "Why do you need me though?"

"Because I told Zack you would help me with the firehose demonstration and activity. He didn't believe I'd be good with the kids by myself."

She chuckled. "And he was okay with me helping?"

I shrugged. "He said I'm less cranky when you're around." Probably because she didn't mind talking to people and letting me be me.

"And when were you going to tell me you voluntold me for this?"

"Um, today?" I offered. "But then you said you were sick."

She laid back against the cushion with a slight chuckle. I stood and lifted the blanket. "Here, why don't you lie down and try to rest."

She turned and pulled her feet up, lying horizontally on the couch. I covered her with the blanket, and my chest felt funny as she stared up at me with a smile.

"Thank you," she mumbled as her eyes drifted closed.

I picked up her bowl and carried it into the kitchen. There were dishes in the sink, a half-cut lemon and an empty tissue box on the counter. I cleaned up and put the dishes in the dishwasher, gave the African violet a little water, and moved into the living room, gathering trash from the coffee table.

I gently placed the back of my hand against Violet's forehead and breathed a sigh of relief that she was no longer running a fever. Hopefully it stayed like that. After I finished cleaning up, I relaxed in one of the chairs across from her, closing my eyes.

A noise roused me, and I opened my eyes to see Violet walking back in from the kitchen. Had I fallen asleep? I sat up, taking in her bewildered expression.

"Did you clean the kitchen?"

"Just put the dishes in the dishwasher and cleared off the counters a bit."

"If I weren't currently sick right now, I'd kiss you." Her brows rose and pink tinged her cheeks. "Like, not literally. I just meant... You know, thank you."

I smirked at the fact that she was tongue-tied. But I definitely wouldn't mind a thank you kiss. Glancing at my watch, I bit back a groan. I didn't want to leave her, but I had to be at the station in the next hour and still had to run home to get my stuff.

I stood and walked over to her, feeling her forehead again. Good, still no fever.

"I have to go."

Her lips turned down into a pout and I smiled, loving that she didn't want me to leave either.

I let my hands rest on her shoulders before slowly moving

them down her arms. "I'm on shift tonight. Call me if you need anything, though. We can swing by."

She shook her head. "I won't need anything."

"If you do, promise you'll call?"

She stared at me, so much uncertainty in her eyes that it was killing me. I wanted to tell her that in a few short weeks she'd become so much more than a fake anything. That I wanted whatever this was between us to be real. I just hoped she felt the same way.

But I wasn't going to say any of that right now. When I told her those things, unless she told me she didn't feel the same, I wouldn't be walking away.

Finally, she nodded and I forced myself to step back. "I'll text you later."

"Okay."

Reluctantly, I made my way out the door and to my car. Determined that the next opportunity I had I wouldn't let the moment to tell her how I felt get away.

Chapter Twenty-Four

VIOLET

I RODE NEXT to Seth in the front seat of one of the FD's utility trucks as he pulled a trailer decorated by the local middle school behind us. The local Boy Scout troop walked in front of us, with Adam and Lyla between us and them as a safety precaution. My job was to toss candy into the crowd of spectators lining the parade route.

I had told Seth I was fine to walk in the parade with the other PD and FD families. But since I had just started feeling like myself yesterday after three days of being sick, he'd convinced me to conserve my energy and ride with him. I was going to have to help him lead the fire hose activity and supervise a bunch of kids, so conserving my energy wasn't a bad idea.

Seth slammed on the brakes just as Lyla lost her footing,

stumbling over something in the road. Adam was quick, reaching out to grab her arm before she could faceplant into the pavement.

"Friends my ass," Seth mumbled under his breath.

I glanced over at him. "What?'

"Those two." He tilted his chin up, indicating the pair in front of us. "I don't buy that they're just friends."

I cocked my head, studying them as Adam held her arm and made sure she was okay. "Why?"

He scoffed before looking over at me. "Trust me, no guy fusses over a girl like that unless he wants to be more than just her friend."

I stared at him, trying to decipher the look in his eyes. Almost like he wanted to say more. It made me wonder how he really felt about me. Because between taking care of me when I was sick and persuading me to ride with him, he'd done his own fair share of fussing over a girl in the last week. But maybe that wasn't what he meant and I was just reading into him being a nice guy.

I smiled, thinking how sweet he'd been, stopping by every day to check on me. James would never have done that. The one time I was sick while we dated, he stayed away because he 'didn't want to catch whatever plague I was incubating.' He really was an insensitive ass.

The truck lurched forward, pulling me from my thoughts, and I turned back toward the window and threw another handful of candy toward a group of kids jumping and waving at us.

Seth raised an eyebrow. "You're going to end up running out of candy before we reach the end."

I opened a new bag of candy, throwing some out to the crowd. "I feel bad when it looks like one or two kids didn't get any."

He chuckled and shook his head.

I finished two more bags just as we made the turn at the end of the marked route. "Look at that. I had just enough."

"Good girl."

I sucked in breath, his words shooting straight between my

legs, and he sent me a smirk. Did he know the effect he had on me? Did he feel it too? And why did we have to be on the clock for an event when all I really wanted to do was try to figure out the answers to those questions.

Businesses along Main Street had an hour to set up for the block party, so we made our way back to the firehouse. I tried not to overthink the way he looked at me, or how the tension grew between us as we made the ten-minute drive back.

Once he parked the truck, I got out and followed him through the bay and out onto the back lot where he began laying the hose out.

"What do you need me to do?" I asked.

He nodded to two large wooden cutouts. "Grab those and set them up down there where the piece of tape is marked on the ground."

Easy enough. I set out the house-shaped boards, both with window cutouts that had flames hinged in the middle. I guessed that was what the kids would aim for.

"Dylan gave me a hard time about all this." I put my hands on my hips and sent Seth a smirk.

"Why?"

"'Cause I'm helping the FD instead of PD."

Seth chuckled. "It's not our fault we have more fun things. No one wants to do pull-ups on a bar."

I raised a brow. He obviously didn't know preteen and teen boys. "You'd be surprised. Boys come in swarms trying to see who can do more than the other."

He shook his head. "Yeah, I could see my brother doing that."

"But not you?" Was he just not competitive? Or did he just not feel the need to show off? Or both?

"Nope." He shrugged. "I probably would have thought it was stupid. If I wanted to work out, I would go to the gym. But my brother would have done it just to show off."

Of course he would have thought it was stupid. I shook my head and placed my hands on my hips. His gaze roamed down to my chest and that tingle in my core was back as he stared at my breasts.

He tipped his chin at me. "Hopefully you don't scare the kids with your skull and crossbones."

I glanced down at my white T-shirt and the hope I had a second ago disappeared. I squared my shoulders, pushing my chest out.

"I can go help PD if you'd rather…" Teasingly I started walking away, heading toward the front of the building.

"Oh no you don't." He grabbed my hand, turning me and pulling me back.

I stumbled and fell into his chest. His arms wrapped around my back, and he stared down at me. My breath hitched as his gaze locked on my lips. That same heat I swore was there a moment ago, that I'd felt earlier when he'd called me a good girl as well as last weekend when we went out with Logan and Izzy, was back. Maybe I wasn't making it all up.

I had convinced myself I'd had too many drinks that night. The few times I'd seen him this week when he'd stopped by to check on me and bring me stuff, I hadn't gotten an inkling of desire.

"Hey, Seth," Jay called. Seth made no move to pull back. He searched my face, reluctance written all over his expression. "Can you help me close off the road?"

His arms dropped and I stepped back.

"Yeah," he called back. But he still didn't move. "I'll be right back," he whispered to me.

"Okay." I nodded.

I wasn't sure what to do while I waited for him, but Zack appeared a minute later with a wide smile aimed at me.

"Thanks for doing this."

I shrugged. "Sounds like it'll be fun. But you know Seth could have handled this all by himself. He's actually pretty good with kids." At least I assumed he was good with other kids, and not just his niece. At least five kids came up to him before the parade, and they knew him by name, lending further evidence to my assumption.

"I know. For someone who's cranky and doesn't like people, he seems to be great with kids." Zack smirked. "But this way he gets to hang out with his girl, too. You make him happy. We've all seen that in the last month."

I opened my mouth to respond, but I had no idea what to say to that. I couldn't deny it because I was supposed to be his girlfriend.

"You better not be giving her a hard time," Seth's voice rumbled.

Zack shot me a wink. "Wouldn't dream of it." He turned and slapped Seth on the shoulder as he passed.

Seth ignored him, diving straight into how this would work. Owen's wife Cece, and Jay's wife Sarah, were manning the information table out front and would send small groups of kids and parents to check out the fire engine before coming out this way for a demonstration of the hose. Then each kid would get a chance—with Seth's help, of course—to aim the hose at the wooden house cutouts to try to knock down the flames.

"So, I just reset the flames for the next kid?"

He nodded with a smirk. "And then get out of the way." He ran his hand down one suspender that covered his tight gray uniform T-shirt and connected to his turnout pants. I never would have thought suspenders could be sexy, but on him they were.

The first two groups went quickly. But the third one was chaotic for sure. Sibling rivalry at its finest. The kids kept fighting and the parents scolded them multiple times. We'd heard their bickering as they approached our area, and I was just hoping the group they were in went quickly.

After resetting the flames for the next kid in line, I stepped a few feet away to wait. Seth turned on the nozzle and helped the little boy hold the hose steady. Just like I expected, he was so good with each kid who had come through. Patient and pleasant and not at all gruff or broody.

The problem children started bickering again, and almost in slow motion, I watched as the boy pushed his sister forward, in turn bumping Seth and the little boy he was working with. The hose shot wildly to the right, hitting me square in the chest. I took a step back from the slight force, and was actually a little grateful for the drenching. The cold water felt good with the intense heat of the day.

Seth got it back under control and finished with the kid. Luckily, the parents of the problem children pulled them away, scolding them for their behavior.

"Sorry, are you okay?" he said, jogging over to me. When I nodded, he added, "Go up to the bunk room. My bag is on one of the beds, it has my name on it. I keep a spare, clean T-shirt in there."

He stared intently at my chest. Was he going to tease me about my skull and crossbones again?

I shook my head. "It's fine. I'll dry."

His brows shot to his hairline as he glanced back up at my face. "You're wearing a white shirt."

I tilted my head and followed his gaze back down to my chest. Oh. Crap. The outline of my bra showed perfectly through the now drenched material. Not only that, but my nipples and the piercings were obvious too. Maybe I should have gone with the padded bra instead of a sheer one.

I looked back up at him. His eyes darkened, making his hazel irises almost nonexistent, and he licked his lips, taking a small step forward. My breath caught in my throat. It was impossible to deny the lust in his eyes as he stared at my breasts.

The sound of kids and their parents came from behind me, reminding me of my current, very public situation.

Seth blinked. "Don't move," he growled before moving out of my eye line. He reappeared a moment later with his turnout jacket and wrapped it over my shoulders.

I smiled. He was being a bit over the top, but just like everything else he'd done in the last month, he was also super sweet.

"I'll be right back." My voice cracked and I cleared it, trying to rid the lust from it.

He nodded and I turned and made my way back inside the station. Trying and failing to not overthink everything I thought I knew. Because there was no way I could ignore the way he looked at me. But what did it mean? And was I ready to find out?

SETH

I was sure seeing her in a see-through white T-shirt, confirming the nipple piercings, would be the thing to bring me to my knees. It was all I could think about since she'd walked away. But that was nothing compared to seeing her in one of *my* shirts. I was doing a shit job of concentrating on the current group of kids we had because my gaze kept drifting to her in those ridiculous cutoffs and fishnets with one of my T-shirts tied at her left hip, showing off just a sliver of skin.

All week I kept reminding myself it wasn't the right time to tell her how I felt and what I wanted. But after today, I wasn't sure I could wait much longer. The need to pull her into my arms and kiss her until neither of us could breathe had become so strong I was surprised I hadn't yet.

Finally, the last group finished, and we were alone once again. She carried the wooden cutouts up and leaned them against the back of the firehouse as I rolled the hose back up.

"So that fundraising dinner I was invited to?" She took a breath before continuing. "I can bring a date."

I froze. This was my opportunity. I placed the hose in the back of the utility truck and spun to face her, trying not to smile like an idiot at her. But I couldn't stop the excitement that sped through me. "Yeah?"

She nodded. "I wondered if you'd be able to go with me."

Hell yes, I wanted to go with her.

She shifted on her feet. "I understand if not. It's not like anyone from Half Moon Lake will see us." My shoulders dropped. "But if you wanted to go with me..." Her shoulders lifted in a slight shrug, and she glanced at the ground between us.

I hated what I had to say, but I was officially done with the fake dating crap. "No."

Her gaze found mine and I cursed the disappointment that stared back at me. Before I could say more, she started talking again.

"Right. No, that's fine." She took a quick breath, trying to brush off what she'd obviously thought was a rejection, before continuing. "It's way too serious to bring a fake date to."

I took a step forward. "Violet—"

"No big deal. Really. I totally get it."

Another step forward. "Violet—" I tried again.

She waved me away. "It was a stupid idea. Not even sure why I brought it up."

I needed her to just be quiet and let me talk. To explain that I wanted to go with her. But in no way as her *fake* boyfriend.

I closed the distance between us and cupped her face in my hands, smirking as her eyes widened, and brought her lips to meet mine.

This time I wasn't holding back. I put everything I wanted to tell her in the kiss. Everything I felt. Her hands came up, holding onto my forearms as I devoured her mouth. Moving, desperate, purposeful. I swallowed down a moan, not sure which of us it came from, and deepened the kiss. Intent on showing her exactly what I wanted. Claiming her mouth so she had no doubts about what this was.

She pulled back, her breath coming quickly, and stared up at me. "Why—I mean...What was that for?"

I brushed my thumbs along her cheeks. "I needed you to stop talking so I could tell you that I don't want to fake date anymore."

Her brows shot up and she opened her mouth to respond.

I placed my thumb over her lips. "Shh, let me explain." I gathered my thoughts and prayed she was ready to hear this. "I want to walk into that fundraising dinner with you on my arm, not as my fake girlfriend, but as my real one." Her breath hitched as her lips parted. "I know you're still getting over James—"

She shook her head frantically. "I'm not. I mean, I'm so over him."

I smiled. "You told me at the beginning of this that you weren't ready to date again, and at the time, I wasn't either. But at this point, I can't keep acting like I don't want this to be real. Because I do. So much." I took a deep breath, knowing I needed to give her space and time if she needed it. "But I understand if you're not ready. If you need more time—"

I barely got the last word out before she was popping up on her tiptoes and pressing her lips to mine. This time, I wound my arms around her back and pulled her tight against me. Her hands threaded into my hair at the back of my neck as we each fought for control of the kiss. She pulled and nipped, and I parted her lips with my tongue, demanding entrance.

A throat clearing nearby interrupted the moment. I pulled back with a growl and glared over at Zack.

He smirked back at me. "A bunch of us are going out after shift. Just wanted to see if you guys wanted to come."

I'd almost forgotten I was technically on shift. In order to accommodate the demonstrations, we'd had to split the crew again and even it out with some volunteers in case any calls came in. I didn't care about going out with the crew. All I wanted to do was to leave here with Violet and find out what her kiss really meant. If I were still in Charlotte, I wouldn't have had to be on shift while helping with an event. But then again, I wouldn't be standing here with Violet either.

"No, not this time," Violet said. "We have plans tonight."

I looked back down at her, worried I'd forgotten something. "We do?"

She nodded. "Yes. Remember? You're coming over to my place." The way she said it had a huskiness to it I was sure I'd never heard before.

Add in the wink she shot me, and a mix of excitement and desire barreled through me at what she was implying. Or at least what I hoped she was implying.

"Okay. TMI. I'm out." Zack turned and headed back into the firehouse.

I reached up and tucked a piece of her hair behind her ear. As much as I wanted her, I also wanted her to know exactly what I wanted—all of her. Whenever she was ready. And not just the physical stuff.

"Violet," I started, searching for the right words. "If you want to take things slow or need more time, just say the word. But I don't want to take you to lunch just to keep up appearances that we're dating. I want to take you to lunch because I miss you and need to see you. I want to pull you into my arms and kiss you because I can't go another minute without feeling your lips, not because someone's watching who can keep the gossip train entertained. I want to spend every night with you because we can't stand to be apart." I searched her face, hoping I wasn't messing this up.

"I want all that too, Seth. I honestly didn't think I would. I worried I wasn't ready to trust someone again. But you're not my ex. In fact, you're nothing like him. And I know that." Her fingers brushed the back of my neck and my eyes drifted shut, letting the sensation take over. "I want to give us a real chance."

Happiness bloomed in my chest. After Lucy destroyed me, I thought I'd never feel like this again. But in just a few short weeks, the way Violet had embraced who I was without trying to change me broke down the walls I'd constructed.

I opened my eyes and leaned down, claiming her mouth once more and wishing I could take her somewhere more private. Lay her down and explore every inch of her body. Find out where all her piercings and tattoos were hiding and trace each one with my tongue.

The alarms sounded inside the station and I reluctantly let her go. "I'll see you tonight after shift?"

She nodded. "I can't wait." Her teeth pressed into her bottom lip and heat flashed in her eyes.

A groan tumbled from my mouth and I leaned down, pressing a quick kiss on her lips before turning and jogging into the station.

Three hours before I'd get to spend all night with my girl. I ignored the knowing smirks the guys were giving me. There was no way I wasn't smiling like an idiot, and I had no intention of changing that.

Chapter Twenty-Five

SETH

I JOGGED up to Violet's front door and rang the doorbell. Having showered and changed at the station as soon as shift was over, I went straight to her place. And even then, it felt like I couldn't get there fast enough.

The door swung open and all the blood in my body rushed south.

Jesus. Adjusting myself, I ran my gaze down her body. The only thing covering her was my T-shirt from earlier. I zeroed in on where her tits pushed against the fabric. It was still hard to believe my girl had her nipples pierced. The thought of making her scream out my name as I tugged on them amped up my anticipation to near unhealthy levels.

I glanced around, making sure no one could see what was

meant for only me, and stepped inside. Finding out if she had anything on underneath became my sole priority.

She moved back and I pulled the door shut, slowly taking her in, wanting to savor every moment of this. A bit of mischief danced in her eyes, like she knew exactly what answering the door in just my shirt would do to me. Her face was free of makeup, revealing a light dusting of freckles, and her hair tumbled down around her shoulders in soft waves.

Fuck, she was so beautiful.

Reaching out, I slid one hand around to her lower back, pressing her against me, and cupped the side of her face with my other hand. "I like you in my shirt."

"Yeah, I don't think you're getting this one back."

"That's fine." I captured her mouth, pulling on her bottom lip, and tangled my hand in her hair. With a gentle tug, I tilted her head back and exposed her neck.

Her fingers dug into my back as I trailed kisses down the delicate skin of her throat. She arched into me, and I moved my hand to cup her breast, feeling her nipple harden through the thin material. I brushed my thumb over the ends of the piercing, the movement making her squirm and moan.

"I like these." I continued toying with the piece of jewelry. "Do they make your nipples super sensitive?"

She nodded and moaned. "Really sensitive."

"Perfect." I ran my hands down her body, teasing the skin of her thighs where the T-shirt ended. "Please tell me you have nothing on under this."

"Guess you have to find out."

I bent down, and with one arm behind her back, I slid my other arm under her knees, lifting her into my arms. "Oh, don't worry, I plan to find out. But first we need a bed. So I can lay you out and explore every inch of your body."

She rested her head against my chest. Desire pounded through my system, but so did something else. Something much deeper. Holding her in my arms like this felt so right. So perfect.

Once in her room, I laid her down on the bed. Running my hands up her thighs, I pushed the shirt higher until her bare pussy was exposed.

"Beautiful," I murmured, moving the shirt up and over her stomach, revealing a piercing above her belly button and a heart-shaped spiderweb tattoo right below her left hip. "Spiderwebs?" This one was similar to the one on her wrist.

She nodded. "I think the patterns are interesting, and no two are the same."

I traced the design with one finger and then continued pushing the shirt up. She sat up and I pulled it over her head.

A groan slipped out between my lips as she fell back on the bed, completely naked, her skin slightly flushed. Her chest rose and fell as she held my gaze, and I couldn't wait another minute to touch her. To taste her. To make her mine.

I pushed her thighs apart and ran my hands up her body, cupping each of her full tits, using my thumb to flick each piercing until she was writhing with pleasure.

"Please, Seth."

Without stopping my assault on her nipples, I leaned down and slid my tongue up her slit. With a flick of my tongue, she trembled. Her hips bucked as I teased her, as I moved my thumbs faster against her nipples, licking and sucking her clit.

"Right there." She threaded her fingers through my hair and tugged on the ends. "Oh my God, I'm gonna come."

I smiled at the surprise evident in her voice. Had no one ever pleased her like this? Pride surged through me at the idea I might be the first.

I flicked and swirled my tongue until she began to rock her hips, pushing her delicious pussy against my face. Her grip on my hair tightened and I fucking loved it. She whimpered and then cried out as spasms shook her entire body.

I loved the way she tasted. Need like I'd never felt before flooded me, and my cock pushed hard against the fabric of my pants, desperate to be set free.

Her movements slowed as I helped her ride out her orgasm. I stood and quickly discarded my clothes, grabbing a condom from my wallet before tossing it on the pile. She leaned up on her forearms and watched me as I rolled it down over my length.

"I want you on top." I needed to make this last as long as I could, and make sure she'd come again. "I want to play with those nipples as you ride my cock."

With a smirk, she sat up on her knees and scooted over on the bed, letting me lay in the middle. "I've thought about getting my clit pierced."

"I like the idea, but it would have to be a woman doing it. No way do I want any man seeing your pussy but me."

She swung her leg over me and braced her hands on my chest. "So possessive." She rocked her hips, sliding the length of my dick through her wetness. "I shouldn't, but I like it."

She raised up on her knees, lining the tip up with her entrance, and began lowering herself down.

Jesus Christ, she felt fucking amazing. I closed my eyes, focusing on the feel of her pussy as she slowly—almost unbearably so—inched down till she was fully seated.

"Fuck, baby." I dug my fingers into her hips, preventing her from moving yet. She felt too damn good. Maybe I was better off flipping her over and keeping control.

She rocked forward and I hissed as my cock slid almost all the way out of her, then groaned when she slammed back down. I reached up and grabbed her tits, using my thumbs to flick the bars of her piercings.

She moaned loudly and I grabbed the end of each one, tugging gently.

"More." She stared down at me. "Harder."

Her movements picked up as I did as she asked, her core gripping me like a vice and contracting each time our bodies slapped together.

I matched her rhythm, thrusting up every time she lowered herself down. I was completely lost in her, the feel of her. The way her soft brown eyes held mine and her hair framed her face. Her desperate little moans. How her pussy clenched around me.

I needed her to come again, quickly, because I knew I wasn't lasting much longer. I moved one hand down to where we were joined and flicked her clit with my thumb.

She trembled and threw her head back. "I can't."

"Yes, you can." I pushed harder and tugged on the bar attached to her nipple. "Come for me again, baby. Let me feel you."

She bounced hard as I flicked and tugged, and then she screamed out as her core tightened around me. I couldn't hold back any longer. My body stiffened and I groaned as the intensity of my climax barreled through my body. I gripped her hips as she rocked over me, pulling out every drop of my release.

She collapsed down onto my chest with a sigh, and I wound my arms around her back, holding her tight to me. I kissed the top of her head and rolled us to the side, slipping out of her. Pressing a kiss to her lips, I brushed the hair away from her face. "Need to deal with the condom."

She nodded and I rolled to the edge of the bed before making my way to the bathroom. When I returned, she lay curled up on her side with her eyes closed. I climbed into the bed and covered us with the blanket. A tiny snore escaped her, and I smiled, gently pulling her into my side.

Five months ago, I was so sure happiness like this again would elude me forever. Or at least for a very long time. Never in a million years did I think this was a possibility. But I couldn't deny I was falling hard for this amazing woman.

Chapter Twenty-Six

VIOLET

WE STILL HAD no new leads in the arson case, so I knew I shouldn't be smiling. But I couldn't help it. Seth had spent Saturday night and all day Sunday with me since we were both off. But both of us had to work today even though it was Labor Day. Technically, I could have taken it off, but with this arson case still not having any breaks, I really needed to watch more footage.

There had to be something we were missing. We hadn't been able to connect either the Taylor kid or his godfather to any of the locations. The godfather wasn't at all helpful when Dylan questioned him either. Straight up defensive and threatened to get a lawyer if we didn't stop harassing them.

My phone vibrated on my desk and I quickly reached for it

hoping it was Seth. Only a slight twinge of disappointment followed when I saw it was Hattie.

> Hattie: Still good for lunch? Can't wait to hear all about your weekend ;)

> Me: I'm not one to kiss and tell.

> Hattie: Yeah, ok.

I smiled and set my phone back down. She knew as well as I did I couldn't wait to tell her everything. Well, maybe not *everything*. Probably not what I did when we were watching a movie. And definitely not what we did on the back deck later that night. Heat rose quickly to my face as I thought about how he'd touched me under the blanket and whispered that I had to be quiet.

I sat up straight and hit pause on the video footage I'd been watching, and honestly, only half paying attention to. My eyes narrowed at the figure wearing a green hoodie. I was pretty sure I'd seen it before.

After searching through the folder of screenshots I'd captured from the other footage of pretty much any person who stood out to me, I found the image I was looking for. Definitely looked like the same person. The build was the same, and definitely stood out to me as a man, but with the hood up and the angle from the back, I wouldn't be able to determine features like skin color or hair.

I stood and went to find Dylan. "I might have something."

He looked up and pushed his chair back. "Show me."

I nodded and he followed me back to my office. I pulled up both images on my computer screen. "Same guy, right?"

"Yeah, definitely could be. Wish we could see his face though."

"It's never that easy."

He scoffed. "Don't I know it. Send me those clips."

"Sure thing, Bossman."

He tilted his head as he looked at me. "You're in an extra good mood today."

I smiled with a slight shrug. I was totally in an extra good mood, but I had no plans on telling Dylan why.

With a shake of his head, he turned and walked back out of my office. I emailed him the clips and got back to watching the footage. Maybe I could catch Mr. Green Hoodie when he wasn't looking away.

~

MY EYES WERE tired by the time I had to leave to meet Hattie. My good mood had faded a bit after watching almost two hours of footage with nothing more to show for it. Not a single sighting of the guy in the green hoodie. It was frustrating, almost like he knew every business and home that had a camera. Like he knew exactly how to go completely undetected.

She was already seated at a table and waved me over. "You're totally glowing," she said as I took my seat.

I chuckled. "I think you're being dramatic."

"You haven't smiled quite like this since Asshole James broke your heart." She bounced in her seat. "Now tell me everything."

Pausing halfway through to order our food, I filled her in on what happened Saturday when I asked him if he wanted to be my date to the fundraiser dinner.

"You're welcome for that, by the way." She sent me a sly smirk. "I'm glad you took my advice, though."

I was glad too. In the back of my mind, a part of me had hoped he wanted to be my real date, but never did I imagine he wanted to be my real boyfriend. Our food was delivered, and I filled her in on some details of Saturday and Sunday as we ate.

"I didn't realize how bad things had gotten with James until being with Seth. He's so attentive."

"I bet. I could tell that when you guys came out for Savannah's birthday. He's observant. Seemed to pick up on your needs even before you did."

I nodded. "I noticed that too, but just thought he did a good job of faking it."

"You know some of the comments on that viral video called this, or at least thought something was already happening between you two."

My body flushed, remembering that day. I wouldn't lie and say I hadn't felt something as I'd buried my face into his neck. But at the time, I didn't want to read too much into it.

"When will you see him again?"

"We're supposed to grab dinner tonight after his shift... as long as he doesn't get stuck there." I fiddled with the napkin in my lap before picking it up and setting it on the table. "I might swing by and say hi before heading back to the station."

I was already missing him and couldn't wait to see him. Plus, who wouldn't be happy about a surprise visit from their new, very real girlfriend.

Chapter Twenty-Seven

SETH

Logan raised a brow at me. "Why are you all smiley today?"

"'Cause he got laid," Zack said without even missing a beat. He didn't even look up from the stack of cards he was busy shuffling.

He had a big mouth. But I couldn't deny the fact that spending almost the whole weekend with Violet made me extremely happy. We'd even made plans to stay overnight at the hotel near the college for the fundraising dinner she was invited to in a couple of weeks. I was really looking forward to it.

"Just deal the cards, Stoer," I snapped.

He chuckled. "Oooh, salty! That didn't take long."

"Yes, because you annoy me."

Zack inhaled dramatically and placed his hands over his heart. "You wound me."

"I'm about to hurt you if you don't deal the damn cards already."

"Fine, fine." He chucked again, but at least he started dealing out the cards.

Jay came up the stairs and tipped his chin my way. "Hey Seth, there's some woman downstairs asking for you."

I sat up straight. "Violet?" The thought had me pushing back my chair and jumping to my feet.

Jay shook his head. "Sorry, man. Not Violet." He shrugged. "Some blonde."

Blonde? I hadn't had any issues with the random women showing up since Violet and I started fake dating a month ago, so I had no clue who it could be.

I made my way down the stairs. Only other blonde I knew…

I stopped dead in my tracks once I confirmed who it was. What the hell was she doing here?

"Lucy?"

She turned, a huge smile on her face. And the complete opposite of how I remember our last moments together.

"Seth." She walked quickly toward me with her arms out. "I've missed you."

I put my hands on her shoulders, stopping her from hugging me. "Lucy, what are you doing here?"

"I came to visit for a few days. I can stay with you, right?"

Was she serious?

She looked up at me and smiled shyly. "I realize I made a mistake. I regret not saying yes and moving here with you and starting our life together."

She was serious. What the fuck. I started to shake my head, but the next words out of her mouth shocked me to my core.

"I'm pregnant."

I didn't know what to say. I just stared at her, wondering if I'd heard her correctly. My grip on her shoulders loosened and she took the opportunity to step into my space, wrapping her arms around my back.

I was going to be a father. And Lucy would be the mother of my child?

Chapter Twenty-Eight

VIOLET

I COULDN'T BELIEVE what I was seeing. There had to be a logical explanation. I knew there was. This couldn't be happening to me twice.

But even as I was convincing myself he had a good reason for hugging a blonde woman I didn't recognize, I turned and walked away. He hadn't seen me yet, and I wasn't ready to find out who she was.

Was I overreacting? Totally. Absolutely. One hundred percent.

But my heart wasn't getting that memo. It was too afraid of being crushed like a bug again.

By the time I arrived back at the station, I had already gone through multiple scenarios to explain what I saw. Maybe she was his sister-in-law. God, I would be the worst girlfriend in the history of girlfriends if he found out something happened to his brother, and I'd resorted to jealousy first. But why wouldn't she call? Would she drive all this way without a phone call? And wouldn't he have told me she was on her way?

Then I thought maybe it was his ex. She realized how much of an idiot she'd been and she wanted him back. Is that what he wanted? They had years together, we'd only had a month. Even though I was sure the heartbreak would be worse than I'd experienced with James, I couldn't blame him if he chose her. But I had no way of knowing if it was his ex. Maybe some deep diving on social media would help me figure it out.

Great. Now I was turning into a Facebook stalker.

I plopped down in my chair and leaned back, closing my eyes. I was officially ridiculous. Yup. Certifiable.

I should just walk back down there. But what would I say? I saw you with some blonde and then ran away.

Jesus. That would go over great.

I blew out a breath and glared at Dylan as he stepped into my office. I swear this better be important, and not dog shit again or some stupid old people feud, because I was not in the mood.

"Uh, I can come back." He took a step back, glancing quickly back over his shoulder.

I sighed. "It's fine."

"Oh boy." He shook his head. "Fine never means fine."

He wasn't wrong. I sighed. "What do you need?"

"Some kids threw fireworks in someone's mailbox last night. Patrol didn't call it in. They didn't really see anything other than a bunch of mailbox pieces. But we should keep an eye on it if they keep it up." He shifted his weight. "Just wanted to put it on your radar."

What in the world? I thought kids were all about playing video games and watching people play video games on YouTube, not starting fires and blowing up mailboxes.

"You good?" Dylan studied me.

I nodded. "I will be." As soon as I figured out what the hell I should do.

I sat there staring at the doorway long after Dylan walked away. I tried to focus back on watching the footage, but I was only half paying attention again when my phone chimed and I lunged for it.

> Hattie: Evelyn was just in here running her mouth about seeing your new man checking into the bed and breakfast with some blonde. I wanted to throat punch her. But why would Seth be checking into a bed and breakfast with some blonde?

Evelyn worked the front desk at the B&B, and I couldn't see why she would make that up. Oh God. But why would he need to check into a bed and breakfast? He had his cabin up on the mountain he was renting.

Dylan appeared again. "Um, Seth is here asking for you. Is that okay? Or should I send him away?"

Regardless of the details, I had a feeling I really didn't want to have this conversation. But whatever it was, I couldn't avoid it forever. Should just get it out of the way. "No, everything's fine. Tell him I'll be out in a minute."

"If you say so." He shook his head and walked away.

I took a few deep breaths before standing and heading that way too.

SETH

"I don't know what you did"—Dylan eyed me suspiciously—"but you are in so much trouble. She said everything's fine."

What the hell was he rambling about? I hadn't done anything. And what did Violet say was fine?

My gaze locked on her as she stepped into the lobby. Shit. Maybe Dylan was right. She definitely looked pissed. But it couldn't be at me.

"You okay?" I asked.

"Yup." She crossed her arms over her chest. Her usual smile nowhere to be found.

I had no idea what I could have done to piss her off. It couldn't have anything to do with Lucy. No one knew who she was, and the only person I had told was Owen. With his history, he was sympathetic and had no problem with me taking the rest of the day off.

"Can we talk?" I tried again as I observed her rigid posture and lips pressed into a tight line.

"Yeah." The simple word held a definite bite to it.

Maybe she was having a shitty day. I hated that I had to give her bad news on top of it, but I also couldn't wait. She needed to know.

"Um, not here?" I glanced around the lobby of the police station. "Can we go somewhere? Maybe the park?" I wasn't sure how she would react, but regardless, I didn't want to have this conversation here with so many prying eyes. "We can sit on a bench and talk."

She sighed. "Sure."

She was so quiet as we walked, and I didn't know what to do with that. She was rarely this kind of eerie silent. "You sure you're okay?"

"I'm fine."

Oh boy. There was that fine again. "Maybe Dylan was right," I mumbled.

"What?" She glared over at me.

I shook my head. Didn't need to piss her off even more. "Nothing, never mind."

I itched to reach out and entwine our fingers as we made our way across the street to the park, but I wasn't sure she wanted that at the moment. Had something happened with the arson case? Whatever it was, she obviously didn't want to talk about it, so I wasn't going to push.

I waved at a bench, and once she sat down, I took the seat next to her. "So, my ex showed up today." Just rip the Band-Aid off, no need to sugarcoat it. "She's pregnant." Violet studied me, her lips parted slightly, but other than that she barely reacted. "She wanted to stay with me, but I told her no and checked her into the B&B."

Her eyes widened and she sucked in a breath. "You didn't sleep with her?"

That was a weird question, and not one I knew how to answer. I cocked a brow at Violet. "Five months ago, when we were together, I did."

"No, I meant today. You didn't sleep with her today?"

"Of course not." What the hell? "Why would you think that?"

"Hattie texted me... Evelyn told her she checked you and some blonde into the B&B."

"Fucking small-town gossip," I mumbled, turning to face her. "Violet, the only person I want to sleep with is you."

"So, you're not breaking up with me?"

Jesus. That was the last thing I wanted to do. "No." I sighed. "But I was worried you'd break up with me."

"Why?"

"Because I'm having a baby with someone else."

She waved that off. "Yeah, but that happened a while ago."

I wasn't about to argue with her train of thought. If she could get past this and we could figure out how to make it all work, who was I to tell her otherwise?

I wrapped one arm around her shoulders and brought her against my chest.

Multiple scenarios ran through my head. I wasn't sure how this would all work out, and I was probably getting ahead of myself, but I knew one thing: if my kid was in Charlotte, then I needed to be there too.

Chapter Twenty-Nine

VIOLET

"So, she just left?" Hattie picked up her margarita, taking a sip.

"Yup." I shrugged, having been just as surprised earlier when Seth told me. I half expected Lucy to try harder to wedge herself between us. "Sounds like once she realized Seth wasn't getting back together with her, she went back home."

"You're handling all this better than I would."

"I don't think that's true. If it came down to it, you would choose to support Dylan over making it about yourself. You're like the least selfish person I know."

Honestly, I didn't see an alternative. Now that we were together and I could admit my feelings, I was quickly falling in love with Seth. Probably had been for the last month. And, when it came down to it, if I wanted to be with him, I needed to be okay with this. It wasn't like he could change what was happening, and he was trying to do the right thing. That had to count for something.

"Thanks. I think." Her brows creased.

I waved her off. "You know what I mean."

"I do." She paused as the waitress appeared, delivering our nachos. "Has he said what he's planning to do?"

"About what?"

"Is he planning to move back to Charlotte?"

"He hasn't said, but I would imagine so." I doubted he wanted to be two hours away from his kid. The idea of him not being here sat heavy in my stomach, but I understood why. I licked the sugar off the rim of my margarita and then took a sip. "He's going back there next week to go to the doctor's appointment with her."

A scoff erupted from Hattie. "Surprised she even agreed to that."

I shrugged. "She might still be holding out hope he'll take her back."

She studied me. "Wait, is that what you think?"

"I don't know." I hated to say yes, but Jesus, he'd wanted to marry her once upon a time, and she was going to have his child. How could I not think that somewhere deep down? "Between sonograms and doctor's appointments, they'll be spending a lot of time together over the next few months. And then, once the baby is born, he'll be there and I'll be here."

Her head angled as her brows pulled together. "Are you not willing to move there?"

It wasn't that I wasn't willing, but it was more complicated than that, wasn't it? Would he be ready for that? His life would already be changing in a big way. "I wouldn't be opposed to the idea."

"Does he know that?"

I shrugged. "We haven't really talked about what we're doing.

It's only been two days. I don't expect him to figure everything out right now."

"Well, yeah, I get that. But he's already had one girlfriend decide breaking up with him was better than having to move. So... I guess what I'm saying is just let him know that you're open to the idea when the time comes."

I nodded. "You're probably right."

"Are you seeing him tonight?" She reached for a nacho from the plate in the middle of the table.

"No. He's on night shift for the next two nights."

My phone vibrated on the table, and I picked it up, smiling as I clicked on the text notification from Seth.

> Mountain Man: I miss you.

> Me: Miss you too.

> Mountain Man: Are you having fun?

> Me: Yeah. Wish you were here though.

> Mountain Man: So glad you said that. Turn around.

I spun around on my stool, catching sight of Seth standing by the bar. I couldn't believe he was here. Was it just a coincidence, or did he come to see me?

He sent me a smile and leaned over, saying something to Adam before making his way toward me. My stomach flipped as his intense stare stayed locked on me, making me feel like the only woman in the entire place. He wore suspenders over his heather gray T-shirt—his signature look when he wasn't in full gear—and something about it caused heat to pool low in my belly.

I let my legs open further, making room for him to step between them. He ran his hands up my thighs and over my hips, settling on my waist. The shiver that raced through me from his simple touch took me by surprise.

"Hi." The smile he aimed at me had so much more behind it than the simple word he spoke.

"Hey," I breathed out, running my hands up his forearms that twitched under my touch. I glanced over his shoulder. "Did Adam drag you here for a food run?"

"No. I volunteered to go."

"You did?" Did he just want to come see me? I chuckled. "I bet the guys all gave you a hard time about that."

"They did at first. Until I told them you were here." He smirked and then took a quick look over at Adam, who was now holding a plastic bag full of what I assumed were food containers. "Wish I could stay, but we'd better get back with the food before a call comes in."

I nodded and he leaned forward, brushing his lips against mine. I gripped the back of his neck, not wanting the kiss to end, but reluctantly letting him pull back.

He pressed a quick kiss to the tip of my nose. "Text me when you get home tonight."

"Okay." I let my fingers trail back down his arms.

Once he and Adam were gone, I turned back to Hattie, who wore a knowing smile.

"You have it bad for that man."

My face heated. She wasn't wrong. I had definitely fallen for Seth Davis.

Chapter Thirty

SETH

"He ran that way," the older man told Dylan. "Into the woods."

Maybe we would actually catch a break this time with an eyewitness. Almost like clockwork, the arsonist had struck again. I wondered if Violet had already made the connection. I hadn't until that moment.

The first one I'd dealt with was at the beginning of May. Then he set Logan's garage on fire at the beginning of June, but there was nothing in July. The one in August happened the first week of August, and now this one was in the beginning of September. I made a mental note to ask Violet when she arrived on scene.

I was dying to see her, but preferably not because she had to come help investigate another fire. The last one didn't go too well. Well... I smiled. Maybe it did. It had brought us together, after all.

I planned to follow her through the house this time and not let her out of my sight. That settled, I tuned back in to the conversation Dylan was having with the older guy who lived across the street.

"Did you recognize him?" Dylan asked.

The man shook his head. "I couldn't see his face. He wore a sweatshirt with the hood up."

"Was it green?"

"It was dark." The guy paused and his shoulders slumped. "I'm sorry, I don't know."

Dylan's jaw locked. I understood his frustration, but it was also why our arsonist liked the early morning hours. It was easier to come and go without prying eyes when it was still dark out.

My feet were moving the second Violet's car pulled up along the curb. I fucking missed her. Between working night shifts and dealing with Lucy, I'd barely seen her in the last two days.

I'd done my best to be kind to Lucy. Open to the idea of talking, but also making it very clear we were not getting back together. Only to have her throw a fit yesterday and go back to Charlotte. I was almost worried she'd freeze me out, decide not to let me go to the doctor's appointment and sonogram. But so far, she hadn't said anything to make me think she changed her mind on that.

The second Violet was close enough, I wrapped my arms around her shoulders, bringing her into my chest. I breathed her in, letting her ground me.

"Rough morning?" she mumbled.

"Yeah." I pulled back and looked down at her. "Rough couple of days."

She gave me a slight nod and I stared down at her. I was still nervous that the situation with Lucy would affect my relationship with Violet. It was so new, and obviously not what she signed up for. But so far, she'd been nothing but supportive and understanding. Would that change when I moved back to Charlotte? Would history repeat itself and another relationship end for the same reasons?

I blinked. Violet was nothing like Lucy, I knew that, but it didn't stop me from wondering how things between us might change once I was living in Charlotte, having to co-parent with my ex.

She reached up and brushed a long lock of my hair off my forehead. Staring into her eyes, everything around us disappearing, I vowed to do whatever I could to make this work. It was almost impossible to fight the pull between us, and I didn't care who saw, I needed to feel her lips on mine. But the chaste kiss we shared wasn't enough to tamp down the need to hold her in my arms and get lost in her.

It didn't matter that I saw her last night for a few minutes, or the fact that it had only been forty-eight hours since we were in each other's arms. The time away from her was torture. Thankfully we only had one more night of this.

A throat clearing behind me made me reluctantly let her go and step back. She brushed past me, and Dylan filled her in on their eyewitness statement and what he had marked for her inside to look at and bag.

I followed behind them until they got to the door, when they both stopped and turned my way.

Dylan cocked a brow, silently asking what I was doing.

"I'm not letting her out of my sight this time. We haven't started the overhaul process yet, and with this dry heat, the fire could reignite easily."

We probably had at least another few weeks of high temperatures and very little rain, which always made our jobs a little harder.

Dylan looked over at Violet. "Please tell me I wasn't this bad when Hattie and I first got together."

Violet chuckled. "No. You were worse."

He scoffed. "Seriously?"

"Totally." She nodded and then moved forward into the house.

"In my defense," Dylan said as he followed behind her, "she did have a stalker trying to come after her."

I didn't care if they thought I was being overprotective. Frankly, I would do this for anyone poking around the scene of a fire before we had a chance to overhaul. But I was definitely making damn sure I did it for Violet.

Dylan showed Violet the few spots he'd marked for her on the first level and left us both inside to go canvas the neighbors.

She squatted down at one of the numbered evidence cards and glanced back at me. "I'm assuming it's pointless to argue with you about following me around."

"That's a good assumption."

She rolled her eyes. "Here then, hold the flashlight on this spot while I collect a sample."

I took the flashlight from her and held it on the spot she'd indicated. "Seems like the fires are always at the beginning of the month."

She nodded. "Not a specific date, but I have noticed it's always between the third and tenth. The BBQ joint threw us off, but now it makes sense why."

"Sucks that the eyewitness didn't get a good look."

"Yeah, and I'm afraid the arsonist is getting bolder. Not being as careful." She finished the second spot Dylan had marked and I followed her into the third room.

"Might be a good thing. The bolder he gets the less careful he'll be."

She put her hands on her hips and glared at me. "Bolder could mean careless, but it can also mean more dangerous. If someone gets hurt or dies because we couldn't catch this guy..."

She didn't finish her sentence. Didn't need to. I closed the distance and pulled her into a hug. "You're doing the best you can."

"Yeah, and sometimes that isn't good enough."

I knew that feeling all too well. You couldn't save everyone, and you couldn't prevent every tragic accident either. You constantly played the what if game in your head.

After a moment, she stepped out of my embrace and went back to collecting evidence. I held the flashlight for her and we both fell quiet while she worked. Our conversation hung heavy over us. It shouldn't, but it surprised me that she dealt with the same thing that first responders constantly dealt with. It made sense, we couldn't save everyone in the moment, but people behind the scenes worked hard to stop bad things from happening again and bring justice to the victims.

She was hyper-focused, meticulous as she examined and collected evidence. Violet was good at, and obviously enjoyed, her job. Would she be willing to leave it and move to Charlotte at some point? I forced my shoulders to relax. I had to remember that we would figure all that out when the time came. There was no use worrying about it right now.

After she was done on this level, I followed her upstairs. "Want to grab lunch later? Or dinner before my shift?" I asked as she moved into the third bedroom after having finished looking around the first two.

I leaned my shoulder against the door frame and crossed my arms over my chest, letting my gaze roam down her body. The tiny leather-like shorts she wore reminded me of that day I pulled her out of that fire.

She spun back to me. "Sure. Let's do dinner. Since I'm starting earlier today, I can leave a little early." I nodded and she studied me as she took a few steps forward, coming to stand in front of me. "And then tomorrow night you'll be off again?"

"Yeah." I reached out and gripped her chin with my thumb and forefinger. "And I can't wait to spend all night showing you how much I've missed you."

Her lips parted with a sharp intake of air. I leaned forward, claiming her mouth. There was nothing chaste or gentle about this kiss. It had all my need for her wrapped up in it.

I pulled back, wishing we were anywhere but in this charred house, and tucked her hair behind her ear. "Want to come up to the cabin tomorrow when you get off? I can make us dinner and we can sit by the fire."

She nodded with a smile pulling at her lips. "You cook?"

I shrugged. "Yeah. Nothing fancy. When I first became a firefighter, I got stuck doing a lot of the cooking that first year, so I had to learn."

"Hmm. Well, dinner at your place sounds great. I can bring dessert."

I gripped her waist and tugged her close. "That's perfect, considering I was already intending to have you for dessert."

"Oh?" Lust flashed through her eyes as her lips parted slightly.

"One hundred percent planning to lay you out and devour every ounce of your sweet pussy until I have you begging to come."

The skin of her cheeks flushed a light pink. "I can't wait."

I pressed a quick kiss to her forehead and stepped back. "Better get back to it before I decide to lay you out right here." I didn't even try to hide my hard as fuck cock as I openly adjusted myself.

Her eyes flared with protest and I chuckled, leaning back against the door frame as she turned back to her job with a slight pout. It was nice to know we were both on the same page, ready for some very intense and intentional time alone together.

Chapter Thirty-One

VIOLET

Dinner last night at The Dock with Seth was perfect as usual. But our time together wasn't nearly long enough. We'd had fifteen minutes in his car afterwards before he needed to head to the station. We took advantage of it by making out like we were teenagers again. He left me so turned on, but with promises of making it up to me the minute I showed up at his cabin that evening.

I squeezed my legs together to relieve some of the tension as I thought about all the dirty things he'd said he was going to do. If I thought it was hot when he said he'd have me for dessert, the way he laid out in detail how he'd use his tongue to drive me to the brink and back was scorching. He was confident he'd have me begging for release. And of course I didn't argue. I wasn't big on gambling, but even I knew that was a bad bet. He hadn't even touched me yet and I was dying to feel his caress. His mouth on me. His cock deep inside.

I pulled down the long driveway that weaved through trees until it opened to reveal a small cabin. My gaze landed on Seth standing on the porch, arms crossed. The sleeves of his button-down were rolled to his elbows, his strong muscular forearms on display.

I got out and slowly made my way up the short walkway, reveling in the way his heated gaze trailed down my body. I'd put extra thought into my outfit, hoping he'd like the plaid skirt and the added sexiness I wore underneath. And I'd skipped the bra, hoping the outline of my nipple piercings that he loved would drive him crazy.

I didn't even have to guess if it all achieved the desired effect, because the second he was done running his gaze over my body and I was close enough, he reached out and pulled me to him. His hand tangled in my hair, and he claimed my lips, walking us backward until my back hit the wooden post of the porch.

His hand slid up my side and cupped my breast, brushing his thumb over my nipple and the piercing through the thin material of my tank.

He broke the kiss, tugging on my hair and exposing my neck to him so he could pepper kisses along the column of my throat. "I hope the no bra thing is only for me."

I nodded. I was sure he didn't want to hear that I occasionally went without one.

"I had a plan." He nipped at the skin above my collarbone, and I arched into his hand that was still toying with me. "Make you dinner and then fuck your pretty pussy until you can't walk."

I really hoped he was changing the order of events, because I did not want to wait any longer to feel him inside me. "And now?"

He hooked a thumb under one of the straps of my top,

lowering it down my arm until my breast was fully exposed. "Now, I want to fuck you right now. Right here."

Being back in the woods, there probably wasn't anyone else around, but the idea of being out here in the open had me so turned on. He tugged on my piercing with his teeth and a bolt of intense pleasure shot to my core.

I clinched my legs together. "What's stopping you?"

"No condom," he grumbled before flicking his tongue over my nipple.

"I'm on birth control and..." I really didn't want to ruin the moment by telling him I'd been tested recently for everything under the sun because of my cheating ex.

He pulled back, staring at me with so much desire in his gaze that his typically hazel eyes were almost all black. I swallowed.

"I trust you." His hand moved to the other strap of my tank, slowly pulling that one down my arm. "Do you trust me?"

I nodded. His mouth latched onto my other nipple, flicking and tugging on the metal bar, driving me higher and higher.

"I'm dying to find out if you're wearing anything under this." He trailed one hand up my thigh and a smirk pulled at my lips when his fingers brushed along the top hem of my fishnet thigh-high stockings. He groaned as his fingers ran over the leather straps attached. "Fuck, baby." He stepped back. "Spin around and put your hands on the railing. I want to see it."

I did as he asked, and a second later he flipped my skirt up, exposing my bare ass, only covered by the leather straps of my garter belt. I glanced back at him over my shoulder. The way he was drinking me in caused my pussy to throb. He looked like a man ready to devour his favorite meal.

He ran a finger under one of the straps and then flicked it against my skin. I pressed my teeth into my bottom lip, trying to stay quiet, but when he did it again, I couldn't stop the moan that left my lips.

He ran his fingers between my folds. "Already so wet and ready for my cock."

"Please, Seth." My body vibrated with need as he used his fingers to spread my arousal around. "You're driving me insane."

"Good." His hands went to the button of his pants, and I couldn't look away as he pulled his thick cock out. "Is this what you want?" He moved his fist up and down, causing precum to coat the tip.

I licked my lips, so ready for him. "Yes, I want you to fuck me. Now."

"I'll fuck you when I'm good and ready." He reached out and tugged on my piercing, eliciting a sharp hiss from my lips. "I'm going to buy you a chain for these." He smirked. "You would like that, wouldn't you? Me pulling on it while you ride my cock?"

I nodded and squirmed as he yanked on the bar attached to my nipple.

Finally, he stepped up behind me, lining himself up with my entrance. I gripped the railing of the porch tighter, waiting for him to push inside, anticipating the delicious ache that his thick cock would cause until I could adjust to his size.

His fingers dug into my hips as he slowly inched forward. "I love how tight your pussy is. How I can feel you clench around me."

"I like the pain," I hissed out through gritted teeth, throwing my head back with a moan as he pushed forward another inch.

"I know you do." He wound my hair around his hand and applied just enough pressure to make my core throb. I was desperate to feel all of him. I rotated my hips and we both groaned from the intense sensation. "You ready for me?"

"Do it." If he didn't, I was going to lose my mind.

He chuckled at the obvious challenge in my voice and then slammed forward. All the air left my lungs as I cried out. I didn't even care if anyone heard me. The mix of pain and pleasure was so perfect, and I wanted more.

With one hand still tangled in my hair and the other on my waist, he pulled almost all the way out and thrust back in. He wasn't gentle as he did it again and again. Our bodies slapped together, and the sound echoed around us.

He let go of my hair and I missed the sensation. Until his hands went to my ass, spreading my cheeks apart, and he pushed this thumb against my tight hole there. I gasped, the sensation shooting straight to my clit, making it throb more.

"You like that?"

"Yes." I shoved back as he chuckled darkly.

"Such a dirty girl, aren't you?" He circled my hole with his thumb, and I moaned, needing so desperately to come. "You'll let me fuck you here."

The conviction in his statement sent a shiver down my spine, and I gasped remembering how big he was. "You might be too big."

"Don't worry, we'll work up to that and you'll adjust. Just like your pussy does."

His tone exuded confidence, and now I wanted him there, too. I'd never been with anyone I trusted enough to explore that with. Not until Seth. But after being with him, even for such a short period of time, I wanted him everywhere.

He picked up the pace of his movements, pounding in and out of me, continuing to apply light pressure with his thumb. My breasts bounced forward and back as he moved. Between that, his hardness dragging against my walls, and his thumb toying with me, I was flying toward the edge.

He spread my wetness around with his thumb and breached the tight hole. I screamed out, the sensation perfect and over-whelming all at the same time.

"That's it, right there." His fingers dug into my ass cheek. "I can feel you tightening around me. Come for me, baby."

He was right. I was so close to the edge. One more powerful thrust and I was falling.

"Oh my God," I cried out, and my body began to tremble as my orgasm hit me. "Don't stop." I matched his powerful thrusts, riding out each wave that overcame me.

"Never want to stop." He pounded harder and faster. "I want to do this forever."

A growl so feral and fierce it was almost impossible to believe I caused it, ripped from his throat. He exploded inside of me, filling me with his release as my body still shuddered from the most intense orgasm I'd ever had.

He slowed his movements and leaned forward, wrapping one hand around the front of my throat and bringing me upright as his cock slipped out of me. He peppered kisses along my shoulder, working up the side of my neck, and I melted back into him.

"Sorry," he murmured in my ear, "I think I made a mess of you."

I chuckled, feeling his cum coating the inside of my thighs. "Yeah. But it was so worth it."

"Definitely worth it." He nipped at my ear. "You can shower and change into one of my T-shirts while I cook dinner."

I nodded. "Okay."

Half dazed and completely sated, I followed him inside, knowing that experience with him was the most intense and satisfying sexual experience of my life. And I couldn't wait to do it all over again.

Chapter Thirty-Two

SETH

I STIRRED the meat sauce mixture as I waited for Violet to join me in the kitchen. I wasn't lying when I told her I could cook, but I wasn't some Michelin chef or anything. I knew how to make a handful of basic stuff, and I liked to grill... and I hoped Violet liked spaghetti.

Footsteps sounded on the stairs, and I glanced through the open archway between the small kitchen and the living room area. Violet stepped into view, wearing one of my FD T-shirts. She stood in front of one of my bookshelves, examining my collection of paperbacks that filled it. It offered me the perfect profile view of her. Her hair was pulled up now into two space buns, and the nerd in me loved it. Without a bra, the T-shirt framed the outline of her tits, dropping down to curve around her shapely ass.

Damn, I was hard again already. I swallowed the groan that wanted to slip from my lips as I thought about how she'd looked earlier, bent over, holding onto the railing as I plowed into her. What was it about Violet? Sex with her was so insane. Intense. Like nothing I'd ever experienced.

I definitely hadn't done anything like what we did earlier. To be so desperate for each other that we'd just start going at it in the open for anyone to see. Even the rough, feral way I claimed her, it was honestly a first for me. But the way she challenged me, admitted she liked the pain, drove me wild, ready to show her I could give it all to her. Whatever she wanted.

I'd never been with anyone like her, and it wasn't just the sex, either.

It was her.

Her confidence.

How she knew what she wanted, what she liked, and wasn't afraid to embrace it. The fact that she could talk to anyone about anything, but could also just sit quietly and listen to music, not feeling like she had to fill the space with words.

How utterly strong she was. She was constantly confronted by her asshole ex, or at least by the fact that he could literally show up anywhere at any time. My mind went back to that first night we went to The Dock. She didn't cower away when he spat hurtful words at her. Didn't give him what he was looking for. She held her own, no damsel in distress there.

And since then, she'd kept surprising me. I loved how she appreciated the little things I did that actually meant something to me. Like giving her a plant and making her a playlist. She didn't just wave it off as lame, dismissing my efforts as trivial or indifferent, and I couldn't wait to do more things that made her smile.

My stomach sank. What if she decided that me moving to Charlotte and having a baby with someone else was too much to deal with? In five weeks, I was already crazier about her than I was in two years with Lucy. What did that say?

"So what are you making?"

I blinked and focused on her question. "Spaghetti."

"It smells delicious." She walked toward me, coming to stand close to my side and leaning over my forearm to smell the contents of the pan.

I couldn't look away, trailing my gaze over her long eyelashes and plump lips. Her eyes met mine, and when she smiled, my chest tightened.

"You're beautiful," tumbled from my lips.

She ran her hand up my arm and I laid the spoon down on the counter, wrapping my arm around her waist and bringing her against the side of my body.

"And you're amazing. I'm seriously the luckiest girl alive."

I didn't know how, after what had happened with Lucy earlier in the week, she still felt like that. But I wasn't about to argue, even though I still worried it might change.

She popped up on her toes, pressing her lips to mine, and I held her to me with one hand on her lower back and the other behind her head. I deepened the kiss, thrusting my tongue in and exploring every inch of her mouth. I wanted her all over again. To lift her up and place her on the counter while I feasted on her pussy.

The sound of water splashing onto a hot burner pulled a groan from my lips and I broke the kiss.

"Go ahead out to the back patio. The table is all set up." Her lips turned down into a pout and I chuckled. "Trust me, I want to ignore the food and just make a meal of you, too. But at some point, we do need to eat. Keep up our strength for all the activities I have planned for us. And this will all burn if I ignore it." I moved my hand around to cup the side of her face, using my thumb to brush along her bottom lip. "But after we eat, I plan to have you begging for my cock again." Using my hand on her lower back, I pressed her harder against my thigh.

Her lips parted with a sharp intake of air, and I shot her a smirk before stepping back and giving her a swat on her ass. "Go. Before I change my mind and say to hell with the food."

She raised an eyebrow, a challenging glint in her eye. Brat.

I tried to push away thoughts of bending her over my lap and slapping her ass before making her come with my fingers.

I failed and adjusted myself, debating if I actually cared if we ate or not.

She chuckled and finally began moving toward the back door.

Jesus fucking Christ. She might end up being the death of me. But what a way to go.

VIOLET

Seth was suddenly acting strange. In the kitchen earlier, he was flirty and ready to have his way with me again. I could see the way he internally argued with himself, practicing some amazing restraint to not devour me right there on his kitchen counter.

But now, as we were finishing our last bites of food, he was definitely distant.

Finally, I couldn't stand the tense silence that had covered us in the last five minutes.

"You okay?"

His head popped up, eyes wide. "Yeah. Fine."

The words were said too quickly, almost like an automatic response. I raised a brow, and he let out a long breath.

"No."

"What's wrong?" I didn't understand what had changed from the time we were in the kitchen together to now.

He hesitated. But then, almost whispering, he said, "I'm scared of losing you."

Oh my God. This man.

I pushed back my chair and got up, going around to sit on his lap. He wrapped his arms around my back and I took his face in my hands. "Seth, I'm not going anywhere."

His head shook slightly in my hands. "You don't know how you're going to feel in four months when this baby comes." He hugged me tighter. "When I'm in Charlotte."

"When *we're* in Charlotte."

His eyes widened as he searched my face. It was now or never to admit how deep my feelings went for him. To make sure he knew.

I took a deep breath. "My feelings for you aren't going to change, they're only going to get stronger." I brushed the hair back off his forehead. "I'm fine doing long distance until we're both ready. But Seth, in the end, I want to be wherever you are."

"You'd be willing to move?" His brows pulled together ever so slightly and a smile tugged at his lips.

I nodded. "Of course." Hattie was right, he needed to hear this. "I'm not Lucy. And you're not James."

"Damn straight. I'm not anything like that prick."

Man, did I know that. They were nothing alike. Seth constantly put me first. My needs. My wants. Showed up time and time again, even when he didn't need to. He was loyal, and even though it seemed like he didn't like people, he still cared about them.

"I know." I swallowed, nervous that it was too early to tell him that I had fallen in love with him. But then again—I smiled—I did just tell him I would move to Charlotte with him so...

"Violet." He threaded one hand through my hair. "I'm so in love with you it scares me. And maybe it's too soon to tell you that, but I don't care. It's the truth."

"You know, I did just say I would move to be with you." I raised a brow. "I wouldn't be willing to do that if I didn't love you too."

The smile that lit up his face was probably the most endearing thing I'd ever seen. He was like a kid on Christmas morning. His grip tightened in my hair, bringing my mouth to his. His lips brushed against mine. Slowly, tenderly, but it quickly turned into more. Needy and desperate. My body heated like an inferno.

He hooked an arm under my knees, and I gasped as he stood, carrying me a few feet to one of the cushioned benches that surrounded the fire he had going. He sat with me on his lap, using his hand on my inner thigh to hike my leg across his while my other leg dangled over his knee. His shirt that I wore rode high up on my thighs. I wasn't wearing anything underneath and, in this position, I was completely open and bare to him.

His hand trailed up under the shirt, going straight to the apex of my thighs. "You're going to come wrapped around my fingers." He ran one finger up my slit, circling my clit, and I bit down on my bottom lip to stop from crying out. "It's just us out here, baby. You don't have to be quiet." He repeated the motion, and this time I didn't hold back. "I love the sounds you make." He pushed two fingers inside me, and I bucked against the palm of his hand where it pressed on my clit. "Look at your pretty pussy. So wet. So ready for my cock already."

I followed his gaze down, watching him thrust in, pressing and rotating his hand against me each time. I couldn't look away, and it just added to the pleasure he was giving me.

He leaned forward and grabbed one of my piercings through the fabric of the T-shirt. The sensation shot straight to my core, and I screamed out. He moved his hand faster as he tugged on the bar again and again.

Just like every time before with him, I shot quickly to the precipice. He was the only guy I'd experienced these intense orgasms with. My fingers dug into his shoulder as I bucked against his hand.

I threw my head back as my body quivered and my core clenched around his fingers. He didn't stop until the last wave subsided and I relaxed against him.

I laid there with my head on his chest, listening to his heartbeat. He held me tight as my eyelids grew heavy and fluttered shut. The warm feeling of utter happiness was the last thing I remembered as I drifted off to sleep in his arms.

Chapter Thirty-Three

SETH

I WAS HAVING the best dream. Violet and I were married and living in Charlotte together. I had shared custody of my son, and together we had a baby girl. We were so happy. It was the life I imagined after she declared she would move to Charlotte with me.

Last night was so perfect. Holding her by the fire as she slept and then untangling myself to go clean up and put out the fire. She stirred awake as I carried her up to bed, and I ended up back inside her before we passed out in each other's arms.

The dream felt so real, and when the dream turned into her and I alone together, it felt even more real as she got down on her knees and took me into her mouth.

I groaned, the feeling of her warm mouth so intense. I didn't want it to end as I fought to stay immersed in the sleepy bliss.

But the sensation of bare skin against my leg made me finally open my eyes.

I looked down my body. *Fuck*. Wasn't a dream.

I reached down and grabbed a fistful of Violet's hair. "I could get used to waking up like this."

She smiled and hummed around my cock, the vibration sending pleasure shooting through my body. She continued back down, taking almost all of me. The base of my spine tingled, and I groaned. I wasn't sure how long I would last if she kept this up. She swirled her tongue around the tip, and I almost lost it.

"Fuck. Do that again."

She did, and my vision went black as pleasure engulfed me. I tightened my hold on her hair, stopping her. Suddenly needing to feel her on my tongue.

"Come here, baby." I pulled her off me.

"I wasn't done." Her lips turned down into a pout. "I wanted to taste you."

"I know, and you're going to, don't worry." I smirked. "But I want to make you feel good too. Turn around and straddle my face. I want you to come on my tongue while you suck my cock."

She rolled her eyes. "So demanding."

"You love it." I motioned her to me with my finger. "Now get your ass up here."

She scrambled up my body and didn't waste any time turning around and getting in position. I grabbed her ass and pulled her pussy down to my mouth, licking and then sucking on her clit.

She moaned around my cock, and I flicked my tongue back and forth, speeding up her movements as she moved up and down my shaft. She swirled her tongue around the tip again, and my hips bucked off the mattress.

I held her tightly against my face, using my tongue harder and faster until she was grinding against me. I was struggling to hold back. Her warm lips wrapped around my cock, sucking me hard, had me close to the edge. But I wasn't going without her, that was for damn sure.

I felt her start to tremble and then dig her fingernails—almost painfully—into my thighs. I bucked up hard into her mouth and exploded down the back of her throat the second she swallowed around me, sucking every last drop from my cock.

She rolled off of me, collapsing onto the mattress, both of us completely spent.

"Well, that was a hell of a good morning," I said, rolling to my side.

She raised up on her elbows. "That was so hot. I think we should do that every morning."

I stared at her. I couldn't agree more. In that moment, I realized that regardless of where I lived—Charlotte or here—I wanted to spend every night and every morning with her.

Chapter Thirty-Four

VIOLET

FRIDAY NIGHT and all day Saturday with Seth had been amazing. Our schedules could be hectic, but it was nice when we both had a day off together. It surprised me how easily we fell into a comfortable domesticity. How natural it felt to be there with him. From making breakfast together to helping him water plants and picking some vegetables he had growing—it all felt so right.

My favorite part of the day, though, was getting to watch him chop wood while I sat on the porch pretending to read one of my spicy romance novels on my phone. It wasn't that I didn't want to read it. I'd had every intention of immersing myself in it. But the way his muscles flexed as he brought the ax down hard on the wood had been too distracting to focus on my book.

But all good things must end eventually, and he was back at

work while I got to do my favorite Sunday chore—grocery shopping. I actually loved going to the grocery store early on a Sunday. No one there but me and some of the town's elderly population.

I picked up some pasta and made my way down the aisle, freezing at the end when a sudden feeling of someone watching me hit. I glanced back down the way I'd just come. No one was there.

Was I losing my mind?

Was this a lingering effect of a sex hangover? Was that a thing? Because the amount of times Seth had made me come in the last thirty-six hours was definitely a first for me. In fact, in the past, I'd had issues. But now I had to wonder if it was more about the person I was with than a problem with me.

I continued my shopping, stopping at the meat section to get some chicken and ground beef. As I reached for a package of chicken breasts, the hair on my arm felt like it was standing up. I shivered—not in the way Seth made me shiver—the feeling of being watched enveloping me again.

I spun quickly, looking one way and then the other. Literally, there was not a single person in sight.

I stood there for a minute, just to make sure, before I finally shook it off, focusing back on the meats.

My last stop was the produce section toward the front of the store. After grabbing peppers, onions, and brussels sprouts, I moved on to the fruits. I weighed the options of cherries or grapes, one package in each hand, raising and lowering them as I decided which one to get. Maybe I'd just get both.

I glanced up and choked back a gasp as I caught sight of someone wearing a dark green hoodie exiting the store. The figure was so similar to the one on the video footage I had scoured from two of the fires. I dropped the bags of berries and sprinted after the mystery man...or woman. Once outside, I froze out on the sidewalk, looking around.

He was gone.

I blew out a frustrated breath and glanced up at the camera

pointed at me. I had to call Dylan and get him down here. I wanted a look at the grocery store's video footage.

Maybe it was nothing. Or maybe it was the arsonist. A chill worked down my spine. He had no problem sending Logan a message back in June when he lit his garage on fire, and it was no secret I was helping with the case.

Did I need to be worried that he was purposely following me, ready to send me a message, too?

One thing at a time. First call Dylan, and then worry about the fact that the arsonist might've been watching me.

I didn't believe it was all a coincidence. In my line of work, those were few and far between.

Chapter Thirty-Five

VIOLET

WHY DID it feel like no matter what we did, we couldn't catch a damn break. Good news was we could deduce the guy following me in the grocery store was likely the arsonist. Bad news? He was careful. Wore a baseball cap and kept his face down and away from where the cameras were the entire time. Just like in the video footage I'd already watched.

And I was convinced more than ever there was no way it was a coincidence. No one goes to the grocery store and walks around with their head down the whole time.

Dylan of course became super paranoid, and I couldn't get him to agree on my suggestion to use me as bait. Instead, he decided to have a patrol car drive by my house regularly. Which brought me back to the conversation I was having with Seth as we laid in bed together, his arm wrapped around my shoulders and my head on his chest.

"It's ridiculous. I don't need a babysitter."

"I'm with Dylan on this one. Better safe than sorry." Seth pressed his lips to the top of my head. "I hate that I have to leave you in the morning to head to Charlotte, but knowing Dylan has someone keeping an eye on you makes me feel better about it."

Probably good that I didn't tell him about that great idea I brought to Dylan. Seth would probably go all alpha protective male if Dylan had said yes to using me as bait. I smiled. Somehow, I hated that idea less when Seth was the one being overprotective.

"Are you nervous about tomorrow?" I was trying really hard not to be jealous that he was going to the baby appointment with Lucy. I wanted him to know I was supportive. "Or excited? Both?"

"A little of both."

"And you're going to stay with your brother tomorrow night?"

"Yeah, since I have off until Thursday. Figured I'd spend the night there tomorrow and come back sometime Wednesday." His arm tightened slightly around my shoulders, pulling me closer into him. "Unless anything else weird happens and you need me back here."

I rolled my eyes. "I doubt anything will happen with patrol making their presence known."

And that was my argument against them driving by or following me. We needed to catch this guy. And he wasn't going to do anything catch-worthy with eyes everywhere.

"Good." His voice was clipped, like he knew where my thoughts went.

I sighed and relaxed into his hold. There was no point in arguing since Dylan wasn't budging anyway.

"Sure you don't want to come with me?"

He'd asked the same question earlier. And he wasn't in the habit of repeating himself. I raised up on my elbow so I could look at him. "I told you earlier, if you want me to go, I will. In a heartbeat."

He searched my face. "But you're ready to catch this guy..." He sighed. "Honestly, I want him caught too. Especially now that it seems like he has his eyes on you."

I'd told him earlier that Dylan and Aiden would be working on pulling footage from a few of the other businesses that sat around the grocery store to see if they could get a glimpse of the guy or maybe what kind of vehicle he'd gotten into. We were doubtful there were any cameras that covered the entire lot, just pieces of it, but thorough was the name of the game in these situations. Regardless, I would be useful at the station tomorrow going through anything they did find.

All that to say, if Seth said he needed me in Charlotte tomorrow, then that was where I would be.

I studied him for a minute before he shook his head. "As much as I wouldn't mind if you went with me, I agree they need you at the station right now more."

It was nice to know he wanted me with him, but it wasn't like I could go with him to the appointment anyway. I would just be waiting at his brother's house until he got back. His practical side would see that as so much wasted time. I smirked at that thought as I relaxed back down on his chest.

"But..." he started, and I tensed, wondering what he was going to say. "The next time I go home to visit, I want you to come with me."

I smiled. "I can't wait." Then something dawned on me. "Does your family know?"

"About you?"

I shook my head. "No. About the baby."

"Oh." His hand stopped its movement up and down my arm. "My brother does. I talked to him the other day. My parents don't yet."

I popped back up on my elbow and studied him. "Do you think they'll be upset?"

"No, the complete opposite." He sighed. "They'll be excited. But I'm afraid they'll think we're getting back together. And when I tell them that isn't happening, I don't know how they'll react. I want to have that conversation with them in person, not over the phone."

I narrowed my eyes. "So you're planning to do that while you're there tomorrow?"

"Yes." He brushed the hair back behind my ear. "And once I tell them that I found someone who I'm madly in love with, they'll understand."

I softened just a hair. "And if they don't?"

"I don't see that happening. But I also don't need their permission or blessing to live my life the way I see fit." He smirked. "I know once they see how crazy I am about you, they'll get it. My mom already suspected even before we were together."

"Huh?" I tilted my head.

"When I went home right before the softball game a few weeks ago, my mom asked my brother if I was seeing someone. Apparently, I couldn't stop smiling like an idiot at my phone."

I stared at him. Somehow that admission shouldn't have surprised me, but it did.

"Don't look so surprised." He chuckled and lifted my hand off his chest, bringing it to his mouth and pressing his lips to the inside of my wrist. "From that moment I asked you to fake date me—probably even before that—it should've been obvious to both of us that I liked you."

"I don't know... You glowered a lot in those first couple of weeks."

His lips pulled up into a smirk. "And now?"

"You still glower." I traced my finger across his chest. "Just not at me."

"Because you make me happy." He covered my hand with his. "Really fucking happy."

His words settled deep in my core, and I smiled as I thought about how different he was now. How much he had surprised me from the beginning. The guy who used the least amount of words possible turned out to steal my breath with the things he would say to me.

I thought back to how this all started. "Good thing for both of us you don't shy away from running into burning buildings."

His fingers tangled in my hair, and he leaned forward and brought my lips to meet his. The gentle, tender way he kissed me was perfect. But I knew, like every other time, it wouldn't take long before it turned to more. The passion that blazed between us just seemed to get stronger with every passing day. And I prayed it would never diminish.

Chapter Thirty-Six

SETH

I LOOKED up at my brother and took the beer bottle he was holding out to me. "Thanks."

Bringing it to my mouth, I took a long drink as I looked out over his backyard. The last time we were here, I was unsure about what to do about my feelings for Violet. Now, given the events of the day, it was the only thing I was sure about.

He tipped his head toward the door. "Shelby has Dani in the bath now, so want to tell me what the fuck happened today?"

"I told you." I swallowed before forcing the words out. "Not my baby."

He huffed. "Yeah, I got that. But also...what the fuck?"

It was a good thing I'd planned to wait until after the appointment to tell my parents. I had hoped we'd get a sonogram picture today that I could take and show them. To say I was grateful I didn't have to have this same conversation with them too would be an understatement.

"She's only four months along, not five."

"So, what? She was trying to use it to get back with you thinking you weren't going to find out or something?"

I shook my head. "Nah. I don't think so. She seemed legitimately surprised. Said she hasn't gotten a period since we were together." I let my head fall forward as I braced my forearms on my thighs. I knew he wanted all the details, but I really didn't feel like rehashing the whole experience. "She was apologetic, and even embarrassed by the whole thing."

The doctor explained missing a period while on birth control for a while was normal. Which we both knew because she skipped quite a few in the time we were together. She even said it was why she didn't think anything of it until she didn't have one for three months in a row. But since she and I didn't use protection while we were together, she'd just assumed it was mine, not the one-night stand she used a condom with. She even asked the doctor if he was sure. What were the chances of birth control pills and a condom failing at the same time?

Apparently crazy shit like that happened more often than people realized.

"So, why do you not seem relieved?"

I should be. I knew most men in my situation probably would be. And if I was being honest, the only woman I saw having my kids was Violet.

"I am..."

"But?"

I didn't know how to explain what I was feeling, or if he would even understand it. "But I'm also a little disappointed." I looked up at him. "That's stupid, right?"

He grabbed the back of his neck and sat down in the chair next to me. His silence told me he didn't get it.

"Five months ago, I thought I was going to have a wife and a kid at some point." I pointed the tip of my beer bottle at him. "The life you have."

The life I'd always imagined for myself. It had been yanked away from me five months ago, and now, in a way, it felt like it had happened again.

"Not all it's cracked up to be," Mason mumbled.

"Don't do that." I narrowed my eyes at him.

He sighed. "It's just hard, man."

"I know." Did he think I thought it was easy? "But still, you're lucky."

"And you're only twenty-eight, little brother. You have time. Marriage is hard, raising a kid is hard."

I wanted that life with Violet. And that was the part that I was relieved about. Because she was the one I wanted to marry. To have a family with.

The need to see her—to get lost in her and hold her in my arms—was so overwhelming. But how would I explain the sadness I felt when the doctor confirmed the baby couldn't be mine. Would Violet understand? Or would she be pissed that I felt that way?

Chapter Thirty-Seven

VIOLET

THERE WAS a soft knock on my front door, and I glanced that way. Ethan had been stationed outside in his patrol car this evening. Maybe he needed something?

I put down the necklaces I'd been working on and climbed to my feet, padding to the door.

I pulled it open, and my mind was struggling to understand what my eyes were seeing.

Seth. He wasn't supposed to be back until tomorrow. Was something wrong?

"What are you doing here?" I studied him and sensed something wasn't quite right. "Aren't you supposed to be in Charlotte?"

His body language screamed uncomfortable as he ran his

hand over the top of his head, brushing the long strands back. I reached out, taking his other hand and pulling him forward, closing the door behind him.

He tugged me closer, and I wrapped my arms around his back. For the first time since I opened the door, his body seemed to relax. He obviously needed this. Not words, but my touch, my physical comfort. As much as I wanted to pepper him with questions, I wouldn't push. He would tell me what happened, of that I was sure, but if this was what he needed first, I had no problem with that.

We stood there embracing until I took his hand and led him to the couch. He sat and pulled me onto his lap, holding me tightly to him with my head nestled under his chin. His hand ran up and down my thigh before disappearing under the hem of the T-shirt I had stolen from him that first night together.

He froze and I leaned back to look at him.

"I—" He searched my face, and I could see he was trying to find the words.

But if he wasn't ready, I didn't need that right now, and I wanted him to know that.

I put my finger over his lips. "We don't have to talk right now."

He stared at me for a beat before the hesitancy disappeared from his eyes, replaced with something much deeper than just desire. A need that I could decipher as more than physical. His hand gripped the back of my head, and he fused our mouths together. We fought for dominance, and when he nipped at my lower lip, I threaded my hands through his hair, tugging at the ends.

He broke the kiss and grabbed the hem of my shirt, pulling it up and over my head. Leaning me back, he shifted and positioned himself between my legs, peppering kisses down the column of my throat and along my breast until he ran his tongue over my nipple.

"Seth," I moaned, arching my back.

He ignored my plea and continued farther down until his beard brushed the inside of my thigh. His fingers hooked into the waistband of my panties, and he pulled them down my legs, throwing them to the floor to join the T-shirt. "Need to taste you." There was zero teasing as his mouth went straight to my pussy, licking me into a frenzy.

"Jesus," I breathed out as my hips lifted off the cushion.

He sucked hard on my clit, and I gripped his hair tightly as he pushed two fingers inside me and curled them. I cried out as his tongue flicked quickly back and forth. My legs shook and my whole body vibrated as wave after wave hit me with such powerful force I found it hard to breathe.

He stood quickly and removed his clothes, staring at me with such intensity I couldn't look away. His gaze never left mine as he knelt back on the couch between my legs.

"You're fucking gorgeous." He ran his hands up my thighs and over my hips, the tip of his cock pushing against my entrance.

Before I even had a chance to take another breath, he pushed forward, entering me completely. I hissed through gritted teeth and dug my fingers into his forearms as I adjusted to his size.

He shifted, laying his body on top of mine and hooking my leg over his hip. His lips brushed tenderly against mine as he began to move, thrusting into me with a deliberate motion. Slow but hard, hitting my clit with each drive forward.

This was torture. But also, just like all the other times we were together, amazing. I didn't want it to end. Reveled in how I felt so connected to him, neither of us needed to use words to explain how we felt. Our bodies in sync, moving effortlessly together, said it for us.

He pulled back from our kiss, just enough that he could look into my eyes. There were so many emotions swimming there, and I wanted to own each one. Needed him to know I was here for all of it.

His fingers bit into my ass as he drove into me and I reached up, brushing his hair back with my fingers latching tightly onto the strands, holding him close.

Our breaths came faster as his movements sped up, and I moaned loudly, trying—and failing—to hold off my orgasm. I wasn't ready for this to end. But there was no stopping it. My core tightened and it tore through me, pulling all the air from my lungs.

He continued to pound into me over and over until his own release overcame him.

"Fuck," he groaned, pumping furiously as he emptied himself inside of me.

He buried his face in my neck, and I wrapped my arms around his shoulders, holding him to me. After our breathing slowed, he rolled us and repositioned himself on his back with my body flush along his side.

I laid there, with my head on his chest, listening to his heartbeat steady, and waiting until he was ready.

"It's not my baby."

I wasn't even sure I heard him correctly, let alone understood the words he'd just said. But once it sunk in, I popped up and stared at him, sure I must have misheard him.

"What?" I asked.

"She's only four months along, so it can't be mine." He scrubbed a hand down his face. "And I know it's fucking stupid that I'm upset about that. I know I should be relieved, and I guess in a way I am, but..."

"Of course you're upset." I searched for the right words to let him know feeling mixed emotions about something like that was perfectly normal. "In your situation, I think anyone would be."

He raised a brow. "Pretty sure most guys would just be fucking relieved."

I rolled my eyes. "Yeah, maybe shitty guys or those who don't want kids. But that's not you. You obviously want kids. And even though the situation wasn't ideal, I know you were excited about the idea."

"You're not mad?"

"Mad?" I stared at him, confused. Why the hell would I be mad?

"Yeah, about me feeling disappointed I'm not having a baby with my ex." He huffed. "God, even saying it out loud sounds ridiculous."

"Are you disappointed because you want to get back together with her and now that won't happen?"

He leaned up on his elbow and narrowed his eyes. "No, of course not."

"Okay then." I smiled. "I'm not mad."

He shook his head with a chuckle. "Why is everything so easy with you?"

"Do you want me to be difficult? Make you feel bad about how you feel? That doesn't seem like something a loving girl-friend would do, but if that's what you need—"

I squealed as he yanked on my arm, pulling me back down on top of him.

"Don't be sassy." He pressed his lips to my forehead. "I love you just the way you are."

"Good." I laid my head on his chest. "I'm sorry...about today."

He was quiet and I glanced up at him. He looked back down at me, more indecision staring back.

"You want kids, right?" He searched my face for the answer I knew he was hoping for.

I was struck silent by his intensity. He didn't even ease into that question. But I wouldn't lie to him. "I wasn't sure, honestly." His face sagged with disappointment, and I quickly went on. "Until you told me Lucy was having your baby. And even though I was supportive, there was a large part of me that was jealous that she was getting to have this experience with you and not me. I can't promise I want them tomorrow or anything, but with you, I do want that eventually."

He smiled and pressed another kiss to my forehead.

After a minute, I sat up and grabbed his clothes off the floor and tossed them at him. "Get dressed." I grabbed mine next. "I'll be right back."

"Why are we getting dressed?" he called after me. "We're just going to get naked again."

"You'll see," I called back from the top of the stairs before disappearing into my room to put on a bra and actual clothes. I smirked. Actually, maybe I'd forgo the bra and drive him nuts.

After putting on jean shorts and a tank top, I made my way back downstairs. He was dressed and waiting at the bottom of the steps with his arms crossed.

"Let's go," I said as I headed for the door and pulled it open.

He gripped the edge and his eyes flared as he zeroed in on my breasts. "Where are we going? And you're not wearing a bra."

"To get ice cream. And I'm aware." I walked out onto the landing.

He stepped up behind me and lowered his mouth to my ear. "I shouldn't want everyone staring at your tits. But there's something about them knowing my girl is kinky and she's all mine that's turning me on."

"So possessive," I teased with a smirk tugging at my lips.

"Only with you." He nipped at my ear, and I had to squeeze my legs together.

"Come on, before they close." I spun and grabbed his hand before moving forward. "You can tell me what actually happened today on the drive there. Ice cream always makes me feel better."

I hoped it had the same effect on him. Or at the very least just going to do something together and talking about what happened would help.

Chapter Thirty-Eight

SETH

I HATED that I was getting off work later than I wanted to. Violet, of course, understood that we had gotten a call that caused us to stay well past when our shift ended. And since I had switched shifts with someone so I could go with her tomorrow to that fundraising dinner, we would have two nights together before I had to be back on shift on Sunday night.

Before I could dial her number to tell her I was getting ready to leave the station, my phone rang and Mason's name flashed across the screen. It was kind of late for him to be calling and I worried something might be wrong.

I slid the answer button over. "Hey."

"She left me."

I could hear loud music playing in the background and wasn't even sure if I heard him correctly. "What?"

"Shelby. She left, man. Gone." His speech was a bit slurred, and I flinched.

Fuck, had he been drinking? "Where's Dani?"

"She took her and went to stay at her parents'." He let out a long breath. "Wants a divorce."

My stomach bottomed out. Jesus. I knew they were struggling, but somehow, I never imagined this.

The talk I'd had with him earlier in the week suddenly hit differently. Mason and Shelby's relationship was the kind I'd always idolized. Until recently they were always happy, and it was easy to see how much they loved each other. In fact, until this last year, I wasn't sure they ever fought. Mason definitely never talked to me about it until recently. Damn. If they couldn't make it work, who could?

Was every relationship capable of failure? And what the hell did two people need to make it work? Because obviously loving each other wasn't enough.

"Where are you?" I bit out.

Could I keep him on the phone while I made the almost two-hour drive back? I didn't want him to get behind the wheel in his state. *Fuck.* Times like these I hated being so far from my family.

I climbed in the car and started the engine. Mason's voice came through the speakers as he answered my question, telling me what bar he was at. I needed to let Violet know I wasn't coming over tonight. I switched over to my text thread with her as I told Mason to stay put.

> Me: Can't come by tonight. Something came up and I need to head home.

> Violet: Everything okay?

> Me: I don't know yet. I'll fill you in later.

> Violet: Are you still going to the fundraising dinner with me?

Shit. I'd forgotten about that for a minute. But I didn't see a reason why I wouldn't be able to make it back for it. I'd get Mason settled, get a couple hours of rest, then head...home?

Home. When did I start considering Half Moon Lake my home? And was it the place, or the people? Honestly, Violet was my home now. Wherever she was, that was where I wanted to be.

Me: Of course. I'll be there.

I put my phone down in the center console and pulled out of the parking lot. "I'm on my way."

"What am I going to do?"

I blew out a breath, not sure I had the answer he was looking for. If it were Violet, I sure as hell wouldn't let her go without a fight.

"What happened?"

"I came home from work, and she already had a bag packed for her and Dani. Asked me not to make a scene, but that she couldn't stay. She said she wanted a divorce. I can't live without her." His voice cracked and I gripped the steering wheel tighter.

I couldn't imagine how he felt. The thought of losing Violet was unimaginable, and I was sure I wouldn't come back from that heartbreak.

Chapter Thirty-Nine

VIOLET

I FINISHED DRYING my hair and glanced at my phone again. I hadn't heard from Seth, and I was getting worried. When he texted last night and said he had to head home I was confused at the suddenness of it, and a little upset at what it meant for my evening, but I knew it had to be for a good reason. Then he texted late, saying he was at his brother's, and everything was fine. He explained what happened and we texted for a few minutes before saying goodnight.

But as the morning went by with no word from him, I was starting to let my thoughts get the best of me. I understood his feelings the other night. It made sense. He'd been excited to be a father. He liked kids and wanted his own, and Lucy was offering that. And then it was all taken away. What if he decided getting back together with her would give him the things he wanted?

I shook my head and put my hair dryer in my luggage. I wasn't going there. James had made me doubt everything, but I wasn't doing that.

Not with Seth. I refused to be that person.

He said he would be here, and I believed him. He never broke promises or let me down. Even when we were only fake dating.

He would come back, and then we would be on our way to the fundraising dinner. We would spend the night in the hotel as planned, then come home tomorrow. I smiled as I thought about the sexy outfit I'd packed for our night away together. He was going to lose his mind.

My phone vibrated on the bed and I lunged for it, swiping open the text from Seth.

> Mountain Man: Not going to make it back in time. Go without me.

What? My shoulders slumped and my stomach revolted as sadness flooded me. I sat down on the bed and stared at the message, praying it would magically change. But it didn't. I tried calling and it went straight to voicemail. Which just ended up causing frustration to bubble up. If he was going to bail, he could have at least called.

This was not the Seth I'd fallen in love with. He would have never let me down. I pinched my eyes shut and chided myself for thinking the worst. Maybe things with his brother escalated and he really couldn't make it back.

At this point I didn't even want to go. Not without him. But the college was expecting me and I didn't want to let them down. So I had to suck it up and make the best of it.

Chapter Forty

SETH

I HUSTLED up the steps toward the door. I'd stayed later than I should have at Mason's, heading straight for Violet's event after leaving my brother's house. He was still a mess, and I had no idea how everything was going to turn out for him, but his situation had cemented even more for me what was important. I hated that I had to leave him, but at least he was sober and he understood this was important, encouraging me to go and that he'd be fine.

I made my way inside and looked around, hoping I wasn't too late.

My gaze landed on Violet, beautiful and sexy as hell in her black lacy dress that ended just above her knees. She stood talking to a woman and a man, and immediately I moved toward her.

The couple's eyes widened as I approached. Maybe I looked like a man on a mission. They nodded in my direction and Violet spun toward me. As the couple turned and walked away, I prayed Violet wasn't angry. But the one thing I'd learned about her in the short time I'd gotten to know her was that she wasn't one to get mad easily. Not unless you took advantage of her easy-going personality, and I had no intention of ever doing that.

She tilted her head, assessing me. After what felt like a lot longer than a few seconds, my shoulders finally relaxed as she smiled brightly at me. "You made it."

I wrapped her in my arms and pressed a kiss to her forehead. "Of course I did."

Did she doubt I would come? I told her I'd be late, but in no way would I not be here.

"I knew you would." A lighthearted chuckle passed through her lips. "Well, okay, at first I wasn't sure. But once the initial shock and doubt wore off and I thought about it, I knew you wouldn't let me down."

I'd made the almost three-hour drive in record time. It would have taken me almost two hours to get back to Half Moon Lake from Charlotte, putting me there later than she needed to leave to get here on time. I could have asked her to wait for me, and she probably would have. And I probably could have made it if the traffic gods were feeling kind, but apparently they had other plans, as evidenced by the wreck on the main highway getting out of Charlotte.

I knew I couldn't ask her to wait, either. That would be self-ish, and this event wasn't about me. That made the decision to come straight from Charlotte a little easier. It would carve off a little bit of time, putting me here a bit late, but still better than the alternative. Luckily, I'd planned on heading straight to her place after shift, so I already had everything I needed in the car when I left the station last night.

Her smile faded. "But, I did try calling after your text, and it kept going straight to voicemail."

"Sorry about that." I brushed a lock of her hair behind her ear. "I forgot my charger and my phone died almost right after I sent you the text."

"I'll admit I was a little worried..."

I cupped her face with my hands. "Sorry I worried you."

I hated that I did, and I knew she meant not only worried *about* me, but also if I'd be here. After her shitty ex, trusting probably didn't come easy. But I would spend the rest of my life making sure she never had to doubt me, and making sure she forgot all about that asshole.

"But I knew if you were able to come, you'd be here."

"There was no way I wasn't going to be here." I looked around, nervous that I had in fact missed her speech. "Please tell me I'm not too late."

She shook her head. "No. They just started seating everyone." With a wave of her hand, she gestured toward the open doors that led into a room set up with fancy, decorated tables.

"Perfect." I lifted my elbow toward her. "Ready?"

She threaded her arm through mine and lifted on her tiptoes, pressing a quick kiss to my cheek. "I love you."

I grabbed the back of her head, holding her close and staring into her eyes. "I love you, too, baby."

She melted into me as I brushed my lips against hers. A moment later, she rested her head against my arm and we made our way inside with the crowd.

"How's your brother doing?" She asked, glancing up at me.

"Not great. He's a wreck." I flinched, not wanting to put a damper on the evening. "But I'm hopeful they'll be able to work it out."

"I hope so."

We took our seats and made introductions with the rest of the couples at the table. She was the only one from her graduating class and, from what I could tell, the youngest one who had been invited to come speak.

Pride bloomed in my chest for this smart, amazing woman

who had stolen my heart one fake date at a time. I never thought I'd be grateful for having to pull someone out of a fire, but I couldn't be happier about how it ended for both of us.

Chapter Forty-One

VIOLET

IN THE ALMOST THREE weeks since that day in the grocery store when I felt someone watching me, there had been no more sightings of the figure in the green hoodie. The case had stalled again, but the beginning of October was coming up, which made me nervous.

Would there be another fire?

I hadn't felt watched or followed again, which was disappointing. For me, anyway. I knew Seth didn't feel the same. We'd been together pretty much whenever neither of us were at work. I'd started thinking he should just get rid of his cabin and move in with me. It made the most sense since he was renting, and I owned mine. But I also wouldn't be opposed to us buying something up on the mountain together either. I definitely would miss watching him chop wood.

He placed his arm around me. "My mom adores you."

I smiled and raised a brow. "Did you think she wouldn't?"

"No, I knew she would."

We sat side by side, watching his niece playing in the yard with his brother and sister-in-law.

I nodded toward them. "I'm glad they decided to go to counseling and try to make it work."

Seth sighed. "Me too."

He'd been worried about his brother that first week after Shelby had left him, and it was like a weight lifted from his shoulders when Mason called and told him they were going to keep trying.

He shifted closer, his lips grazing my ear. "Got you something."

"You did?" I cocked a brow. It couldn't be another plant. He'd just given me another one last week.

He held up his hand in front of me, a chain dangling from his fingers.

"A necklace?" I reached out and placed my open palm under the chain, letting him drop it into my hand. Definitely not a necklace. I smirked as I held it up, pinching the two barbells with little spiders hanging from them and a chain connecting the two pieces. I leaned in and kissed his cheek, whispering, "I can't wait to wear this later."

"You like it?"

My cheeks heated. "Of course. I love it." Only Seth would buy me jewelry for my nipple piercings. But I love that he embraced my kinks and never made me feel weird for them, unlike other guys I'd dated in the past who shall forevermore remain nameless.

The door to the house slammed shut, startling me, and I closed my fist around the barbell part of the chain and brought my hand down to rest on my lap just in time.

His mom stood there smiling at us. "That's a pretty chain."

Shit. I glanced at Seth who just stared at me, smirking. Asshole.

"Yeah, Mom, it's for one of her crystal pendants that she makes."

Lying to his mom, now. Great. I guess it was better than telling her it was for my nipples.

"Those are so pretty." She sat down in the rocking chair in the corner. "Seth sent me your website. I'm trying to decide which one I should get. You suggested rose quartz for Shelby earlier. What do you think I need?"

"Umm." I assessed her, tilting my head. She hadn't complained of anything specific this evening, so I wasn't sure what she needed. "Clear quartz is a master healer, and you can't go wrong with amethyst or citrine. Labradorite is popular for anti-aging..." I cringed. Did I just imply his mom was old? Awesome. "But I don't have that one. I could always look into getting it if you wanted it, though."

Oh my God, Violet, just stop talking.

She waved that off with a flutter of her hand. "Don't go through the trouble. I think women should embrace their age. And I love the color purple." She smiled, glancing over at Seth. "Amethyst has always been one of my favorite gemstones—especially since both my boys were born in February—so maybe I'll order one of those." She glanced up toward the sky. "But I do love the sun, and didn't you mention earlier that citrine was like the sun stone? So I don't know..." She took a quick breath and looked back at me. "Maybe I'll order one of each."

I loved how his mom tended to ramble like I did sometimes. It all made sense why Seth wasn't bothered by it, and even seemed amused at times.

Mason appeared in front of us, hands on his hips and a glare aimed at Seth. "Did you tell Dani we could go get ice cream after dinner?"

Seth chuckled. "I did not."

Heat crept up my neck as Mason looked down at Dani just as she came up beside him.

"Violet said we could," she blurted.

Mason slowly turned back to me with an eyebrow raised. "Is that so?"

"Sorry, I'm a sucker for ice cream." I shrugged. "Besides, she did that cute please face that Seth said was hard to say no to and he was right, I couldn't say no."

"We can take her if y'all don't wanna go," Seth offered, shooting me a smirk.

Shelby joined the group, looking at Mason with renewed hope in her eyes, her smile filled with anticipation. "We haven't been to get ice cream in forever."

Mason stared at her for a beat before his lips pulled up and he nodded. "Yeah, we haven't." He turned back to the group. "Alright gang, let's load up."

"Maybe your dad and I should stay here." His mother worried her bottom lip between her teeth. "You know the doctor wants us to watch his cholesterol."

"The place we go to has a sorbet, and I think frozen Greek yogurt too," Mason offered.

"Please, Mimi." Dani folded her hands together under her chin, giving her grandmother the same expression she'd used on me earlier.

"Now, how can I say no to that?" His mom stood and held the little girl's hand as they walked inside.

I chuckled. Apparently, I wasn't the only one affected by the cute please face. Seth stood, offering me his hand, and I stuffed the chain I was still holding into my pocket before taking his hand and following his family inside.

This trip had gone perfectly. Much better than I expected. Part of me worried about them accepting me knowing that less than six months ago he had asked Lucy to marry him. But literally from the moment we'd arrived, I felt nothing but welcomed.

Going home to visit my parents would be harder since it

required us to take more time off and either fly or road trip it. Hopefully we could make it work before Thanksgiving, when they were coming to us in Half Moon Lake.

The more I thought about it, the more I wanted to make that trip home happen sooner rather than later. For the first time in any of my relationships, I was excited about the idea of bringing someone home with me. Showing them that side of my life made forever seem that much more real. Thinking back on it, there was no one I'd been that sure about until now.

Until Seth.

Epilogue

SETH

WE ALL CLIMBED out of the truck and went through the routine of stepping out of our turnout gear and getting it set back up for the next call. Today had been one stressful call after another, including a fire and two vehicle collisions.

As the guys made their way up the stairs, I froze, catching sight of Violet walking up to the open bay doors. Happiness spread through my body, just like it did every time I saw her.

I jogged the few feet toward her. "Hey, baby."

"Hi." She smiled up at me as I pulled her into me.

"What are you doing here?"

"Just wanted to stop by and see you." Her hands laced around my neck.

I loved when she stopped by unexpectedly, and whenever I was off during the week and she was at work, I did the same thing.

"Surprised you're not still at the station working on the arson case." Like clockwork, we'd had another fire. This one at the beginning of October.

She shrugged. "Not much we can do. Lyla didn't get a good look at the guy. I've gone through the footage we collected from around the scene and no sign of the green hoodie guy either."

I could tell she was feeling discouraged. Maybe she needed me to take her mind off everything for a moment. I glanced up the stairs, making sure none of the guys were still hanging around, then grabbed her by the hand, pulling her further back into the bay, behind the rig.

Bracing my hands on either side of her, I leaned down and claimed her mouth. Her fingers dug into my sides as I deepened the kiss, slipping my tongue inside. The kiss quickly accelerated from a lit match to a blazing fire. It was always the way it was for us. Passionate and desperate, like we could never get enough of each other.

I got lost in her. In her lips. Her touch. I almost didn't hear the radio until the familiar voice broke through the haze I was in.

I broke the kiss, pulling back as I heard the distress call coming through one of the radios sitting on the table at the bottom of the stairs.

Fuck. I moved closer that way and my stomach bottomed out as I listened to Kyle Williams reporting that their ambulance was just involved in a wreck. Lyla was injured and unconscious. He was requesting a transport for their patient and another unit for Lyla.

I looked up as Adam barreled down the stairs, the rest of the guys following behind.

I turned back to Violet. "I have to go."

She nodded and I gave her a chaste kiss before heading toward my gear. It wasn't only that Lyla was one of us, but she was important to Adam—even if he still hadn't admitted it, we all knew.

If Violet were hurt, I'd be there, and so would the rest of my team. There was no way we weren't heading out. Because I'd bet money on the fact that Adam was in love with the woman he insisted on calling just a friend.

Ready to find out what happens with Adam and Lyla? Make sure to preorder the next book in the series!
The Line of Fire

More By A J Ranney

Half Moon Lake Series:

Always Yours (book 1)

Wishing to be Yours (book 1.5)

Impossibly Yours (book 2)

Imperfectly Yours (book 3)

Bravely Yours (book 3.5)

Recklessly Yours (book 4)

Half Moon Lake Heroes: The Red Line

Bravely Yours (book 0.5)

Playing with Fire

Out of the Fire

The Line of Fire

Calling a Cease Fire

WRITING AS GRACIE YORK

Goldilocks and the Grumpy Bear

Tumbling Head Over Heels

Along Came The Girl

Peter Pumpkined Out

Back Together Again

Ghost Shoes

Follow Me

Come be apart of my Facebook Group.
AJ's Book Nook

Find me on social media:
Instagram.com/a.j.ranney
Facebook.com/ajranney19
tiktok.com/@ajranney3
Goodreads.com/AJ Ranney
http://www.ajranney.com

Note from the Author

Dear Reader,

THANK YOU for reading *Out of the Fire*. Seth and Violet were a fun pair to write. Seth with his grumpy quietness and Violet is so different than what I normally write. Both were great in their own ways.

Next I'm working on Adam and Lyla's story and I'm so excited for this friends to lovers romance!

I appreciate each and every one of you. It's only because people like you read our books that authors like me get to publish them.

Check out my website for bonus content and stay up to date with latest releases.

Love,
AJ Ranney
www.ajranney.com

Acknowledgments

Like always, I need to thank my husband first. He has been one of my biggest cheerleaders, is always willing to listen to what I write, and has done bedtime with the kids more times than I probably realize. I appreciate your eagerness to help me when I'm stuck and your willingness to let me read to you.

And then to my kids, who are always curious about what Mommy is writing. And yes, you still need to wait until you're eighteen to read them. But by then I doubt you'd want to!

Jenn, I know you're sick of my stories by the time we get to this part! Regardless, thank you for dealing with my constant *how do I fix this?* questions and talking me down every time I'm ready to burn everything I write. You're always willing to read and edit multiple times, hold my hand when I need it, and tell me to just do it when I need that too. But above everything you've done, your friendship has meant the world to me.

A HUGE thank you to my author friends who have supported me in so many ways, whether through encouragement or reading my stuff: Annie Charme, Kat Long, Jenni Bara, Brittanee Nicole, Daphne Elliot, Kristin Lee, Amanda Zook, Alexandra Hale and many more!

Also to all my beta readers: thank you for always willing to read and give feedback!

Cami, thank you for all the graphics, reading and helping find teaser lines and the phone calls to chat and get organized. I appreciate all your help!

Michelle, a HUGE thank you goes out to you. Every

comment you left that made me stop and think, even when I wanted to push back. Your guidance really helped shape and mold this book. Thank you for always willing to answer questions or help me talk something out!

Holly, as always, thank you for being my sister, even if not by blood—and to my mom and mother-in-law: You have been so supportive throughout every step of this crazy journey!

And finally, thank you to the rest of my friends and family who have helped or supported me. I used to think it took a village to raise little humans, and that still holds true, but it also takes a village to write and publish a book!

About the Author

A.J. Ranney lives in Maryland with her ever-growing zoo, including two kids, two cats, an attention-loving dog, a bunny, a cricket-eating lizard, and her lovable, well-meaning husband. She likes to leave the chaos of her real world behind and lose herself in a steamy romance novel. Her passion for reading romance prompted her writing journey, leading her to create relatable happily ever afters that come from her own dreams and experiences.

She loves coffee, sushi, wine, and her family. Not necessarily in that order. Her inner peace comes from the water, always relating to her zodiac sign, the Pisces. It's no wonder the small town she created in her stories is situated on a lake.